More Prais

"Entertaining, profound, [...] *Serafina!* shows the marve[...] their apparent marginality, [...] Perfectly attuned with the novel's spirit and rhythm, Gregory Conti's elegant translation prompts the rediscovery of this jewel of Italian literature."

—Serenella Iovino, author of *Ecocriticism and Italy: Ecology, Resistance, and Liberation*

"*Oh, Serafina!* is a bizarrely beautiful fable for the ages. Thanks to the deft work of translator Gregory Conti, this tale of industry, lust, mental illness, and ecological sensibility is a most welcome addition to the small but growing canon of Italian environmental literature available in translation."

—Monica Seger, author of *Landscapes in Between: Environmental Change in Modern Italian Literature and Film*

"Fifty years ago, Giuseppe Berto wrote his fable of ecology, lunacy, and love against the backdrop of the industrialized Italy of his day. But books, fortunately, outlive their occasional contexts. In Gregory Conti's flawless translation, *Oh, Serafina!* shines as a tale that belongs even, if not especially, to our own time."

—Federica Capoferri, coauthor of *Badlands: Il cinema dell'ultima Roma*

Oh, Serafina!

Titles in the **Other Voices of Italy** series:

OVOI

Other Voices of Italy: Italian and Transnational Texts in Translation

Editors: Alessandro Vettori, Sandra Waters, Eilis Kierans

This series presents texts in a variety of genres originally written in Italian. Much like the symbiotic relationship between the wolf and the raven, its principal aim is to introduce new or past authors—who have until now been marginalized—to an English-speaking readership. This series also highlights contemporary transnational authors, as well as writers who have never been translated or who are in need of a fresh/contemporary translation. The series further aims to increase the appreciation of translation as an art form that enhances the importance of cultural diversity.

This book embodies many of the qualities that OVOI holds dear, surprising readers for its themes and topics that are just as relevant and valid today as they were fifty years ago, when the book first appeared in Italian. It is a modern-day fable that speaks a transgressive and progressive language set in a world where the protagonists suffer the alienation of being outcasts for simply loving each other without preconceived notions of class, status, or mental health. Their love of nature casts them further to the margins of a society that is wholly and solely focused on bourgeois profits and disregards the beauty of creation. This forges the pair into an archetypal duo resembling the first biblical couple in an uncontaminated Eden but with a Franciscan flavor transpiring through the love of birds. The abundant irony characterizing *Oh, Serafina! A Fable of Ecology, Lunacy, and Love*, which this brilliant translation renders beautifully, adds literary flavor to a text that could otherwise be a manifesto for the ecologically concerned or the neurodivergent.

Oh, Serafina!

A Fable of Ecology, Lunacy, and Love

GIUSEPPE BERTO

Translated by Gregory Conti

Rutgers University Press
New Brunswick, Camden, and Newark, New Jersey
London and Oxford

Rutgers University Press is a department of Rutgers, The State University of New Jersey, one of the leading public research universities in the nation. By publishing worldwide, it furthers the University's mission of dedication to excellence in teaching, scholarship, research, and clinical care.

Library of Congress Cataloging-in-Publication Data

Names: Berto, Giuseppe, author. | Conti, Gregory, 1952- translator.
Title: Oh, Serafina!: a fable of ecology, lunacy, and love /
Giuseppe Berto; translated by Gregory Conti.
Other titles: Oh, Serafina! English
Description: New Brunswick: Rutgers University Press, [2023] |
Translation of Oh, Serafina! Fiaba di ecologia, di manicomio,
e d'amore. Rusconi Editore, 1973.
Identifiers: LCCN 2022030283 | ISBN 9781978835740 (paperback) |
ISBN 9781978835757 (hardback) | ISBN 9781978835764 (epub) |
ISBN 9781978835771 (pdf)
Subjects: LCGFT: Novels.
Classification: LCC PQ4807.E815 O513 2023 |
DDC 853/.912—dc23/eng/20220707
LC record available at https://lccn.loc.gov/2022030283

A British Cataloging-in-Publication record for this book is available
from the British Library.

Copyright © 2023 by Giuseppe Berto Estate. Published
by arrangement with The Italian Literary Agency
Translation © 2023 by Gregory Conti

rutgersuniversitypress.org

Contents

Foreword

A Personal and Planetary Tale: Giuseppe Berto's Bizarre Environmental Story

Although written fifty years ago for an Italian readership, *Oh, Serafina! A Fable of Ecology, Lunacy, and Love* (*Oh, Serafina! Fiaba di ecologia, di manicomio e d'amore*) speaks across time and place to contemporary readers around the globe. Through its bitter irony, which is also present in most of Berto's literary production, the novel emphasizes the importance of both ecological awareness and a reconsideration of societal attitudes toward mental illness, themes that are unique to this text.

Italian writer Giuseppe Berto (1914–1978) was born in a small town near Treviso, in the Veneto region of Italy, and grew up in a country dominated by fascist ideology. His father, a former police officer, assisted Giuseppe's mother with her millinery business. As many teenagers of that period, Giuseppe, at age fifteen, became a member of the Opera Nazionale Balilla, the Italian Fascist youth organization, whose goal was to educate young people about the ideals of Fascism and train them for possible future military service. Following the Fascist prioritization of education, Berto's father compelled him to complete high school and enroll in college. Prior to entering college, however, Berto enlisted in the Italian army, continuing his active participation in the fascist project.

In 1935, when Italy invaded Ethiopia, Berto left the University of Padua and enlisted, receiving multiple commendations for bravery. After returning to Italy and graduating with a degree in art history in 1940, Berto published his first creative work, a short story (*La colonna Feletti*, 1940) in *Il gazzettino*, a local Venetian newspaper, that recounted the events leading to the deaths of four of his fellow soldiers in the Ethiopian war. The autobiographical nature of this story is an aspect that will characterize Berto's future works. When Italy entered World War II in 1940, Berto's patriotism, driven by his fascist education, prompted him to re-enlist. In 1942, he was sent to fight in Tunisia, but the Italian military campaign failed disastrously, resulting in many casualties and imprisonments. Berto was captured in 1943 by Allied troops and transferred to a prisoner of war camp in Hereford, Texas, where he was detained for three years. Interestingly, despite the harsh conditions of the camp, Berto came into contact with American literature, particularly works by Hemingway and Steinbeck, which helped shape his own style. During his imprisonment, he began to question his involvement with Fascism and his participation in its the conflicts, exploring these themes in the writings he drafted in captivity that appeared in literary pamphlets he and his fellow prisoners created. During that time, he completed an initial draft of both a collection of short stories, *The Works of God and Other Stories* (*Opere di Dio*), later to be published by Macchia, and his novel *The Sky Is Red* (*Il cielo è rosso*), published by Longanesi in 1946, one of the most prominent publishers in Italy even today. *The Sky Is Red* was a commercial and critical success both in Italy and abroad due to its status as one of the first novels to describe the tragedies of World War II. It was awarded the Florence Prize for Literature (the Premio Firenze per la letteratura) in 1948, selected by a committee of the most respected writers of that period. In *The Sky Is Red*, a story of the consequences of the U.S. bombing of Treviso told through the eyes of four children, Berto depicts the suffering of the innocent during conflict and grapples with feelings of his own regret and responsibility in the war.

With this book, Berto was categorized as a member of the neorealist movement that emerged after World War II. Neorealist works narrated the struggle of the antifascist movement, the guerrilla warfare of the resistance, the conditions of Italian society in the aftermath of World War II (particularly in the south), and accounts of those who endured concentration and work camps. Berto's text defies tenets of neorealist writing, however. Whereas neorealist texts are grounded in real events, Berto, having been in Texas at the time of the bombing of Treviso, had no direct knowledge of the experiences narrated in his book (he describes certain places in Treviso as having been bombed that were not). Therefore, his work can be interpreted more as an allegorical depiction of the trauma sustained by any victim of conflict and crisis and the resulting inequity of conflict itself. Additionally, whereas neorealist writers place their political engagement front and center, Berto had fought with the Fascists, not against them. Even though through writing the book he began to process his feelings of guilt and the negative impact of his participation in fascist nationalism and colonialism, he never publicly disavowed his fascist past. Therefore, ever since he entered the scene of Italian literature, Berto was never embraced by intellectual and literary circles, making his specific role challenging to identify.

Berto's next work, *The Brigand* (*Il brigante*) published in 1951 by Einaudi, was not as successful as *The Sky Is Red*; it sold poorly and was highly criticized for the quality of writing and its overly explicit Marxist ideology. Around 1954, Berto began to suffer from an anxiety disorder that severely affected his literary production, leading to no fiction publications over the next ten years. During this time, his only income came from working as a journalist and screenwriter. Interestingly, his most successful novel, *Incubus* (*Il male oscuro*) published in 1964, was a direct result of the journals his psychoanalyst encouraged him to write as part of his therapy. It was not until the publication of *Incubus* that Berto was nationally and internationally recognized as one of the most innovative and experimental authors of that period, creating a space for him in the canon of Italian literature. In addition to being a bestseller, *Incubus* was awarded both the Premio Viareggio and the Premio Campiello, two of the most prestigious literary prizes in Italy. *Incubus* utilizes stream of consciousness as its narrative style, focusing on Berto's difficult relationship with his father, brought on in part by his father's death; the conflict he experienced regarding his own sexuality; his obsession to become a successful writer; the struggle to find doctors who could help him overcome his anxiety; his evolving spirituality; and the solace he experiences as a result of leaving his family and moving to the Calabrian coast to live in solitude and in closer contact with nature.

The themes of death, psychological struggle, spirituality, and the desire to escape society and reconnect with nature are also key themes in *Oh, Serafina!*. Published in 1973, this book is part of the second phase of Berto's production after the publication of *Incubus* and the improvement of his mental health. Originally written in the form of a screenplay, *Oh, Serafina!* won the Premio Bancarella in 1974 and was turned into a movie in 1976. It is the second fantastical allegory that Berto wrote; the first, *La fantarca*, published in 1965, is a science fiction story describing the arrival of a spaceship in southern Italy meant to save the last remaining Italians. Here, too, we see autobiographical elements (the protagonists escape from society to find a better world), biblical and religious themes (the story's connection to Noah's Ark), and satirical elements (the description of planet earth as divided into two giant blocs, West and East, parodying the Cold War).

These themes are further refined in *Oh, Serafina!*. The theme of escaping society and finding solace in nature, which is central to *Oh, Serafina!*, notably allows Berto to express a fierce skepticism toward the Italian economic boom of the '50s and '60s. Although rapid industrialization leading to economic development was still celebrated in the '70s, Berto was among those who criticized the material wealth brought by unchecked economic development. Whereas ecological issues connected to the economic boom were only partially addressed by these movements, they are, instead, at the heart of Berto's tale. Traditional criticism of industrialization by writers of that period focuses on the dissolution of the social fabric, in particular the exploitation of human and natural resources. For example, in the works of Paolo Volponi and Italo Calvino, environmental degradation is connected to human alienation inside the unnatural spaces of cities and factories. The human is always at the center of Berto's texts, but he also concentrates on the role of nature and the possibilities that an egalitarian relationship between humans and nature can bring. In other words, by showing how the well-being of nature corresponds to the psychological and physical well-being of humans, Berto does, in a sense, emphasize the arbitrary nature of the separation between the two realms and demonstrates the need to actively reconsider this divide.

Oh, Serafina! is in dialogue with two central texts of the Italian literary canon. The most important and most crucial is the *Canticle of the Creatures (Cantico delle creature)* by Saint Francis (1224). In fact, the life and actions of the protagonist, Augusto Secondo Valle, are modeled after the life of Saint Francis. As is reported in many hagiographies, Saint Francis was able to speak with birds, a practice Augusto Secondo shares. This can be interpreted as a call for humans, who are experiencing a separation from the natural world, to rebuild a dialogue with nature, specifically to listen not only to the cries of fellow humans alienated by traumatic transformation of the means of production but also to the cries of fellow creatures. The connection with Saint Francis's *Canticle* is in its recognition that both animals and natural environments are our companions, an awareness that inspires both ecological ethics and ecotheology. In fact, this more compassionate and open multispecies relationship is presented in this fantastical story *not* as fantasy or as philosophical (an expectation of the genre) but as a spiritual engagement with nature. It is not a coincidence that this ecospiritual conversation between human and nonhuman life at the center of the tale is also at the center of Pope Francis's recent encyclical, *Praise Be to You (Laudato si'*, 2015). This key religious text is also inspired by Saint Francis's life and text and connects theology to ecotheology, inviting us to consider the planet as the common home of many different creatures, all of whom have value in the eyes of God.

The second key text that connects Berto's work with the Italian literary canon is Giacomo Leopardi's *Eulogy of the Birds (Elogio degli uccelli*, 1824). Here, birds enjoy a harmonious relationship with the natural environment, while humans embody a harrowing separation from it. This triggers, in humans, a melancholic condition and the constant desire to bridge the gap between the natural and the artificial. In *Oh, Serafina!*, as in *Eulogy of the Birds*, birds symbolize what a non-exploitative, peaceful relationship would look like. In this context, Berto depicts a society that carelessly interprets Augusto Secondo's practice of building a dialogue with the birds as an indication of mental illness. However, it is, in fact, this alternative spirituality and misunderstood frame of mind that allows Augusto Secondo and other characters to reconsider their superiority over nature. In other words, since human intelligence and rationality is often considered evidence of human superiority that leads to our separation from nature, thus resulting in environmental degradation and human isolation, the rebuilding of this relationship requires an alternative way of thinking, feeling, and acting, which might be interpreted—as it is in the story—as eccentric, bizarre, or loony.

These environmental themes are as relevant today as they were fifty years ago when *Oh, Serafina!* was first published, if not more so. Unsurprisingly, the 2021 report on mental health and climate change by the American Psychological Association as well as several studies recently published in psychology and psychiatry journals worldwide have demonstrated the increasingly negative impact of environmental degradation on mental well-being. Therefore, this text speaks to contemporary audiences through the ways Berto deals with the anxiety resulting from ecological crisis and deterioration, particularly his ability to convey these serious and complicated themes in an ironic and comical narrative voice that translator Gregory Conti has rendered beautifully in English. In the interview excerpt present in the first edition of *Oh, Serafina!*, Berto stated the following: "*Oh, Serafina!* was only supposed to be a subject for a movie. I wrote it and gave it to some of the most important Italian producers to read. They didn't buy it because they didn't see anything in it. Then I got the idea of making it into a book, because I did see something in it." *Oh, Serafina!* is a fable that comes from a specific space and time, an industrialized area of northern Italy in the '70s, that, through this translation, holds value by allowing a global audience to reflect on its current and future role on an endangered planet.

Matteo Gilebbi
Dartmouth College

Translator's Note

Sometimes things come together in your life in ways you never would have expected and bring you joy. That has been the case for me with this translation.

In the fall of 2013, I was invited by one of the then future editors of Other Voices of Italy, Alessandro Vettori, to teach a course on literary translation for students studying Italian language and literature at Rutgers University. Toward the end of the semester, Alessandro asked if I would be interested in translating *Oh, Serafina!* by Giuseppe Berto. I didn't know the novel and didn't know much about Berto, but I was indeed interested, because my wife, Roberta—like Berto, from the region of Veneto—had spoken about him often and with great enthusiasm. So on my return home to Perugia, I took down the book from our bookshelf, in its first edition from 1973, and started to work.

From then on, my personal connections to Berto, and Augustus the Second, only got thicker. I realized that Berto was writing *Serafina* in 1972 when Roberta, whom I had not yet met, was beginning her career as a psychotherapist in the Italian public mental health system. At the time, Italy was in the process of transitioning from residential public mental hospitals—*manicomi*—to neighborhood outpatient clinics, and Roberta spent part of her time seeing patients in the provincial public mental hospital in Perugia. Five years later, in 1977, as a student in the Yale Law School clinical program, I started my (brief) legal career representing patients at the Connecticut Valley state mental hospital in Middletown. Still later, in 1983, when Roberta came to visit me in Massachusetts, she came with me to meet the patients I was assisting at the Metropolitan State Mental Hospital in Waltham as a supervising attorney in the Boston College Law School clinical program. Alessandro Mantini, Augustus the Second's "venerable attorney" could have been me, and Augustus one of my clients. I had never come so close to translating my own personal experience.

Giuseppe Berto also had some personal experience that he could draw on in creating the fable of Augustus and Serafina. He suffered from frequent bouts of mental illness— anxiety, depression, hypochondria—from which he found relief in psychoanalysis. He then put what he learned in analysis to work in his writing, developing a complex stream of consciousness narrative voice, most notably in his 1964 masterpiece *Il male oscuro* (translated into English by William Weaver with the unfortunate title *Incubus*, in 1966). In *Oh, Serafina!* Berto uses a similar voice in a comic vein.

Also like Augustus the Second, Berto had an experience of involuntary confinement. In 1943, while fighting for fascist Italy in North Africa, he was captured by the Allies and sent to a prisoner of war (POW) camp in Hereford, Texas, where he was held until February 1946. His time as a POW also served Berto in his literary career. In his nearly three years in Texas, he wrote his first two novels, *Il cielo è rosso* and *Opere di Dio*, which were published on his return to Italy and later also in English (*The Sky Is Red* and *The Works of God*, both translated by Angus Davidson). Finally, Berto also used his time as a POW to become an avid and insightful reader of contemporary American literature, starting with Steinbeck and Hemingway and continuing for the rest of his life. That may or may not explain why, as I was translating Augustus the Second's eerie and absurd therapy sessions with Doctor Caroniti, I kept hearing echoes of one of my favorite novels and films of my teenage years, Ken Kesey and Miloš Forman's *One Flew over the Cuckoo's Nest*.

As I said at the outset, everything came together this time around. I hope it does for you, too.

Gregory Conti

Author's Note

I wrote this book because I was short on cash. It often happens that I'm short on cash: I don't earn very much, I'm an improvident spender, and the government makes me pay too much in taxes. Usually, I resolve these money shortages by working for the movie industry. That's what I wanted to do this time too, and actually *Oh, Serafina!* was only supposed to be a subject for a movie. I wrote it and gave it to some of the most important Italian producers to read. They didn't buy it because they didn't see anything in it. Then I got the idea of making it into a book, because I did see something in it. I'm not at all regretful about writing it; in fact I've decided to publish it. It is certainly not a book that is extraneous to me. I put a lot of my humor into it, which I learned through some long, hard suffering. I also put in some of my *pietas*, as Latin writers called it—that is, my being happy about what strikes me as good and my being sad about what strikes me as wicked, and that is something I learned quite easily, by making mistakes. Of the themes that are found to be constant in my works, there is only one that is missing here, the sense of death, but this is a fable, and the characters in a fable are not afraid of death because, as everyone knows, they will live happily ever after.

The protagonists of the story are not completely invented. Augustus the Second is inspired by a lumber merchant who, some years ago, wrote to me about his pain from an Austrian mental hospital. And Serafina, with her incredible piffero, and her even more incredible baggage of sin and purity, I met one day in Rome, in the neighborhood around Piazza Navona.

Giuseppe Berto

Oh, Serafina!

Chapter the First

*In which a factory is presented,
two of its owners are eliminated,
and there emerges a third,
who will be our hero.*

There was once—and probably there still is—but who knows how much it will have changed by now, a button factory by the name of FIBA. It had been founded in 1920—that is, in an era of unquestioned and universal enthusiasm for technological progress—by an extraordinary man whose name was Augustus Valle.

At a certain point in his life, this man had placed, on the right side of his house, which was a rather large building and already a bit antiquated, with an acre of gardens in the back, a sort of villa, but with the air of a farmhouse rising up in the countryside around Milan, more or less in the area of Sesto, there, in a word, he had deployed in a large long structure, which had formerly been a barn, around thirty workers, men and women, along with some German machines which, at the cost of more than a little noise, manufactured buttons, of bone and mother-of-pearl. He had, moreover, placed in another room off to one side, which was called Administration, a desk, some bookshelves, another smaller desk, a bookkeeper by the name of Traversi, a secretary by the name of Rosa, at the time adolescent and pretty, and he had called the whole thing FIBA.

Why Augustus Valle had set himself up making buttons, about which he couldn't have cared less, rather than airplanes, about which he was utterly mad, nobody ever understood. That is, he used to say that making buttons was nothing but a prudent first step on the road to making airplanes, so much so that, to him, the acronym FIBA actually stood for Fabbrica Italiana Bottoni e Aeroplani (Italian Button and Airplane Factory), but he never succeeded in achieving his goal, in part because, instead of making money with buttons, he frittered away a lot of time with the airplanes that a wealthier friend of his was building in a hangar on the outskirts of Lower Bergamo. Between Augustus Valle and flying machines there was, it could be said, a sort of arcane bond, or metaphysical connection, and in truth the good man had survived an incredible number of crash landings in beet fields until, in July 1944, he died in Piazza Cordusio, in Milan, under a rain of bombs, dropped, naturally, from an airplane.

On his deathbed, Augustus Valle, by means of a last will and testament that was capricious but, it was said, more or less legitimate, named as heir to all his property, both real and personal, not his own son Giuseppe, who was declared the simple usufructuary, but rather the four-year-old son of this

Giuseppe, named Augustus like himself, but called even at the time, by way of distinction, Augustus the Second. Why the first Augustus, in establishing the line of succession to FIBA and the adjacent house as well as the acre of gardens in the back, had wanted to skip a generation, may perhaps be understood somewhat by going on with this story, but in the meanwhile the meek Giuseppe Valle, for all the years that he lived, until, practically speaking, just a short time ago, had to engage in a constant struggle with his wife, Belinda Sassi Valle, who wanted him to challenge the will.

"But what does it matter to you whether the owner is me or our son Augustus the Second? Aren't we all part of the same family?"

"That's not true in the least," Signora Belinda rebutted spitefully. "That one there is a Valle; he's certainly not a Sassi."

This was a base and mean distinction, given that the person making it was, after all, a mother, but nevertheless, from a certain point of view, Signora Belinda was not that far off the mark; that child of hers, Augustus the Second, as he was growing up, gradually revealed his, one might say, monstrous, exclusive, and without a doubt intolerable resemblance with this grandfather, Augustus the Founder.

Signora Belinda, obviously, being rather far removed from poetry, had never loved her father-in-law. On the contrary, she had hated him, and since, on the wall behind the desk, in Administration, they had hung a big photograph of him with his bushy mustache—and, what's more, a little votive lamp, almost as though he were some kind of saint—she began to make trouble, demanding that the photograph be removed. This never happened, not surprisingly, and the image of the founder remained in its place, more and more laden with years, dust, and in the end, even with dignity, while it did happen that, little by little, Signora Belinda pared back the frequency of her visits to Administration until she finally never set foot in there again. This created displeasure for no one, not for the by now elderly bookkeeper Traversi, not for Signorina Rosa who was already gliding her way along from forty to fifty, nor, much less, to the usufructuary Giuseppe Valle, who had discovered in Administration a place where he could take shelter from the insolence of his wife.

So the years went by. FIBA remained as it was, a modest little factory, steadily aging, with its acre of gardens, whose trees, planted by some unknown ancestor, grew ever larger. All around it, instead of trees, what grew up were factories and houses, more and more factories and more and more houses, until there was no more empty sky and no more seasons, and the people worked all the time cursing the murderous heat and the murderous cold, and on Sundays they drove for two or three hours in the car to go and see, almost always in Switzerland, what clean air was like. In short, all around FIBA, and without FIBA doing anything to deserve it, the economic boom had exploded.

Little Augustus the Second, meanwhile, like the trees and the houses, was also growing. He embodied, however, his unconscious elective inheritance, gradually developing the mysterious tendency to become the spitting image of his grandfather, founder and aviator. Eventually, if someone had erased the mustache on the portrait on the wall of Administration, or if Augustus the Second, who was old enough by now to grow one, had grown a mustache of his own, nobody would have been able to distinguish the one from the other.

Augustus the Second had been a melancholy and solitary little boy, as one can easily imagine given the kind of mother he had happened upon. As a grown-up he continued to be a loner and didn't talk much to people. With birds, on the other hand, he talked a lot and more than willingly, always placidly, and sometimes even cheerfully.

There were already thousands upon thousands of birds in the trees in the gardens behind FIBA, and others kept on coming, attracted by the place's reputation and even more by the loving care of Augustus the Second, and anyway they didn't have many other alternatives, given that all around the gardens, for kilometers and kilometers, there was nothing else by now but chimneys spewing forth gloomy gray smoke. Some birds, owing either to recklessness or misfortune, had strayed into it and had, it seemed, perished. In any event, no one had ever seen them again.

In the gardens, on the other hand, they still lived a pretty good life. There were trees with very long limbs and thick foliage. There was a small melodious fountain with a tub, and there was, naturally, all the food they could eat, because Augustus the Second never left them without grain or millet. There were birds of all species and dimensions, but for the most part, as is only natural, they were passerines or songbirds, and many of them lived there all year round, while others left with the onset of cold weather to return once winter had passed. Some of these birds, perhaps the most important, or the indigenous species, or the most adept—by sensibility or acoustic perception—at communicating with humans, even had names; odd names like Balco or Pausento but also common names like Pietro or Paolo, and naturally, they answered not only to a whistle but also to their names humanly pronounced, as long as it was Augustus the Second who was pronouncing them. After all, at least in those parts, he was the only one who cultivated such habits.

So, Augustus the Second, by now having reached the age of thirty-three, was out in the gardens chatting with the birds, while inside the house, his parents had launched into one of their usual fights. It was started, as was to be expected, by Signora Belinda who, looking out on the gardens from the living room window, had glimpsed her son with a couple of turtle doves on his head and five or six finches doing a sort of dance on and around his shoes, and she immediately took offense. Really quite something, this Signora Belinda. As if it were possible, looking out on the gardens, to see Augustus the Second involved in any other activity. Malicious troublemaker that, come right down to it, she was, she started shrieking at her poor husband, "I can't stand it!" she shouted. "He's going to kill me! Why don't you go out there and give that jerk a good punch in the face?"

His mother's shouting also reached her son and his birds, but it seemed that both the one and the others were used to it. "There they go again," Augustus limited himself to saying sweetly.

And the birds, in agreement, said, "Cheep, cheep, cheep."

They were not bothered, either by Giuseppe Valle's response or by the rest of the fight.

"That jerk out there," her husband answered, naturally, in a loud voice, "that jerk out there, if you really want to know, reached the age of majority a while ago, and he is the boss around here, in law and in fact. If he wanted to, he could throw you out, and I don't understand why he doesn't."

"Throw me out? Me? Whoa. But are you really so sure that you Valles don't have a few crackpots in the family?"

"Crackpots in our family? Ours? Ooohh! Remember that your grandfather died an alcoholic. And your great-grandfather as well. And your uncle was part of the Fascists' march on Rome!"

"But that son of yours out there, who's a total fool, just where did he pop out from? It's obvious he's a Valle and not a Sassi."

"Better a Valle than a Sassi. The Sassis, if you really want to know, make my skin crawl."

"So I make your skin crawl too, is that what you're saying?"

"You, too, yes, you make my skin crawl, too."

Then came the sound of the first broken vase or plate, followed by volleys of indistinct shouts and more broken vases and plates. The birds, even the ones perched on tree limbs, started to show signs of anxiety. "There, there," Augustus the Second reassured them. "It'll be over soon. Listen up now. He says . . ."

Right on cue Giuseppe's voice rang out, "That's it. I can't take it anymore! I'm going to throw myself off the bell tower!"

"And now," Augustus the Second murmured to the birds, "she answers . . ."

Right on cue came Signora Belinda's response: "Go ahead and jump, if you think you're brave enough!"

Then the door slamming, with broken glass.

Augustus the Second, without disturbing the birds still sitting on his head, followed with a gaze of impotent compassion the massive figure of his father running across the grass on his way, presumably, to take his pain and suffering to Giacomo Ballosta's tavern. On past occasions that's how it had always gone.

This time, however, Giuseppe Valle resisted the temptation of a glass of his favorite Barbera wine, slipped inside the little door to the bell tower, and a few seconds later showed up among the church bells, knocking them together with all the force he could muster. His intention, in all likelihood, was to fill the piazza below with people, but at the time the people were at work, and the only ones who came out of their houses were Giacomo Ballosta, the priest, the town hall employees, and old Maria Busecca, who, by the way, was blind. There weren't many onlookers, down there with their noses in the air, and for a second Giuseppe Valle must have painfully perceived the enormous disproportion between what he was about to do and that sparse assembly. Nevertheless, he pulled himself together and launched his last message to the world: "Get married!" he shouted. "Get married, dumbshits. Then just wait and see how well things turn out for you!"

He threw himself down headfirst and ended up, naturally, dead as a doornail. A bloody spheroid plopped down in the churchyard, with no more worries.

"Crazy," commented matter-of-factly the town hall messenger Eriprando Bottecchia.

"That's easy for you to say," Giacomo Ballosta pointed out, full of understanding. "What else was there for him to do?"

Signora Belinda, true to form, rushed to the scene, looked down at the heap of bones, and said as though to herself but speaking loud enough so that at least those closest to her could hear, "You had to have it your way. . . ."

Finally, Augustus the Second arrived. He looked down at his father so decidedly defunct and didn't say a thing. The idea came into his mind that if he had had wings, maybe he would have pulled it off, but that, after all, it was better this way.

Chapter the Second

In which a funeral is held,
flung open to the future.

Giuseppe Valle was not a decedent who inspired profound feelings of loss. Nevertheless, FIBA closed for a couple of days of mourning and its employees and factory hands went along to swell the crowd at the funeral, which was a modest funeral but religious. In fact, the Valles being a highly regarded local family, it had been established that poor Signor Giuseppe had lost his footing and slipped off the bell tower without any intention of jumping. Otherwise, as a suicide, he couldn't have been buried on consecrated ground.

Signora Belinda had draped herself in grief, every piece of widow's garb imaginable, but more than pain, her face displayed spite, or even contempt, as though she were annoyed by the circumstance that her husband had taken his leave in such an expeditious manner.

Augustus the Second was dressed in mourning, too, black suit and white shirt, on which, however, he had placed, rather curiously, a blue silk bow tie with white polka dots. Since a tie, albeit a bow tie, could hardly be associated with birds, that polka dot bow tie exhibited on the occasion of a funeral was interpreted as being just another of the more than a few extravagances of young Augustus the Second, though pure extravagance it was not, and this was not lost on Signorina Rosa, who, on seeing it, gave a start, and her decrepit cheeks tinged with red. It was said that Signorina Rosa, who in her youth had been so pretty, had remained a spinster because of a secret and unexpressed love for the first Augustus, the founder, and while it may be that this was no more than a bit of gossip spread by people accustomed to busying themselves with other people's affairs, more even than their own, the fact remains that Signorina Rosa remembered everything there was to remember about the first Augustus, even the detail that he had always worn a blue polka dot silk bow tie. To tell the truth, anyone who wanted to could easily have come to know that. All you had to do was look at the portrait of the founder hanging in Administration, in which he wore, for all to see, a polka dot bow tie. But by this time, whoever bothered to look at that portrait?

Anyway, the silk bow tie wasn't the only thing worthy of note that Augustus the Second produced during the course of the funeral. He raised eyebrows over bigger things, and in fact, it happened that right in the middle of the church ceremony, heedless of the wafting incense and Gregorian chant, and who knows maybe even in rebellion against the Dies Irae, he fixed his gaze insistently on one particular female fanny, very well shaped and prominent, which wasn't even right in front of him but a bit off to the side, so that, in short, it was all too evident that he was staring at just that.

At first, this behavior did not fail to cause alarm or even to provoke a bit of disconcertion, but then those in attendance, who were for the most part workers from the factory, concluded that one could manifest his pain over the loss of his father in whatever way one wished, even by staring at a nice female ass, and they turned, barely sparing a thought for the deceased, to the question that had been vexing them for two days now: From now on, who was going to be running the show? The mean mother? Or the lamebrain son?

Their quandary was resolved in a hurry the next day, when FIBA reopened its gates. Two workers went into Administration, equipped with a stepladder, and started taking down the portrait of the founder with his mustache and polka dot bow tie. The new bookkeeper, whose name was Armando Cusetti, a handsome dandy prone to swagger because he knew how to adjust accounts for VAT, the value added tax, was beaming with satisfaction, while Signorina Rosa, as always on such occasions, was resisting an acute attack of colitis. Accordingly, she got up to go to the toilet but also not to witness the sacrilege, and on her way out the door she almost ran into Augustus the Second, still in his black suit and polka dot tie.

"Stop right there!" he shouted with unsuspected verve to the two in the act of removing the founder.

"Actually," one of the two tried to object, "Signora Belinda . . ."

"Signora Belinda isn't in charge of a damn thing around here," Augustus the Second declared. "I'm the boss!"

"Fine with me, that's for the two of you to work out," grumbled the workman and hung the portrait back in place.

But it wasn't over yet because right after that, four more workmen came in, two with a photograph of the just deceased Giuseppe Valle, and the other two with a huge reproduction, also a photograph, of a celebrated fresco by Giotto, or at least generally attributed to Giotto, of Saint Francis in the act of preaching to the birds.

The hanging of these two new figures had still not been completed when Signora Belinda burst into Administration, shouting, "Who had the audacity to go against my orders . . ."

Augustus the Second thrust himself in front of her. "Woman, don't break my balls," he said succinctly.

Signora Belinda looked him up and down, breathless and still incredulous. Then she glanced at the portrait of her deceased husband and the one of that other one preaching to the birds. But with a forceful shove, her son sent her toward the door, shouting, "Out of here! Out!"

Signora Belinda tried to resist. "What are you doing? How dare you hit your mother! Don't you fear the wrath of God?"

"Out! Go back home to your knitting!" Augustus the Second ordered her, undaunted, with such authority that mean Signora Belinda obeyed without another word.

Augustus the Second stood erect, his legs spread wide in the middle of Administration, savoring his triumph. Then he walked briskly over to bookkeeper Cusetti and said to him with astounding resolve, "I'd like to tour the factory."

The bookkeeper sprang to his feet with so much zeal it could have been fake. "I'll summon the foreman Romeo Radice forthwith," he whispered, already on his way.

While he waited, Augustus the Second turned his head to look again at his grandfather, his father, and Saint Francis, by now all hanging on the walls. And all at once, humbly, Signorina Rosa rushed over to him, took his hand, and kissed it repeatedly, almost with insistence, saying, "Bless your soul, just like your grandfather, bless his soul. He too wanted his women in the kitchen. But the times were different back then."

"For me, the times haven't changed," Augustus the Second declared. "And here nothing is to be changed, aside from what has changed already. Everything as it was at the time of my poor grandfather."

"Bless your soul!" Signorina Rosa said again and went back to kissing his hand.

Then the bookkeeper came back in with the foreman Romeo Radice. "At your orders, sir," he said respectfully.

Augustus the Second looked at him, decided he didn't like his face but that there was nothing he could do to change it for him. "Let's go," he said.

In the shop, which still looked a lot like the old barn, some thirty or so men and women were busy churning out buttons, of bone and mother-of-pearl, from antiquated machines that made lots of noise. From time to time, foreman Romeo Radice gave an explanation, but Augustus the Second quickly realized that all this didn't matter at all to him. He yawned continuously and revived a little only when he shot a glance through the window out toward the gardens. His birds were out there; at times he thought he could see one of them flying around, but then it disappeared. "These machines make too much noise," he said to the foreman. "They scare my birds."

"They're old, sir," said the foreman with a gesture of resignation.

Augustus the Second felt even more resigned than him, and he didn't say another word on the subject. He looked out at the gardens; he longed to go out there. "Fine," he said. "Good job. I urge you to make sure that everything continues as before, as things were at the time of my grandfather, bless his soul."

"We still haven't seen the packing and shipping department, sir," said the foreman.

"Couldn't we see it tomorrow?"

The foreman made an eloquently doubtful gesture. "The workers might not take it very well. These yes but them no. It's right next door; it won't take a minute."

Augustus the Second resigned himself to suffering another minute and he let himself be led to the packing and shipping department. And once he had gone in there, he came up short because there was just one woman working there at a table, and since she had her back to him, he could easily confirm that she was the owner of the sensational rump that had so enchanted him the day before during the exequies in the church.

Almost as though she'd been called by the gaze of the owner, the woman turned around, and her face was lovely, too, even though it, too, was round and a little vulgar.

When she recognized the owner, she smiled and made a bow in a rather clumsy attempt to show her refinement.

Augustus the Second, however, was too confused to notice, so confused that he rushed out the door. But once outside, he got hold of himself and asked the foreman, who was still with him, "Now who does that gorgeous ass belong to?"

"To my sister, Palmira Radice," the foreman responded conveniently.

Augustus the Second fell back into a state of confusion and this time to a degree that was irreparable. "Not that one . . . the other one . . ." he managed to blurt out.

The foreman wouldn't have it. "Really, sir, there was only one that I saw."

Chapter the Third

In which Augustus the Second, for love, makes his mother cry, and both make a distressing resolution.

After his vigorous exploit on day one, Augustus the Second, already the owner and now also the new managing director of FIBA, limited himself to keeping his mother away from the factory. Other than that, he stopped into Administration a couple of times a day at most, while in the various production departments, especially the packing and shipping department, he avoided setting foot. He preferred spending his time as he did before, in the gardens, looking after the birds, ever more numerous and ever more in need of a patron like himself. The megalopolis, in fact, was ever more infested, more and more congested with chimneys spouting grimly colored poisons, less and less visibility, and less and less air to breathe. The Lombards steadfastly resisted all the enticements of plans for the industrialization of the south, all the solicitations from the government, all the pressure from the political parties, anything as long as they could stay right there, in the land where, in the final accounting, they had been born, to put up factory after factory, and keep right on "polluting," as those who had been to the United States at least once would say.

Caught in the middle of all this were, above all, the birds, which besides breathing badly and seeing worse, couldn't even find anything to eat anymore. No more fields where they could go pecking seeds and fruit, no more gnats hovering in the air to snap up on the fly, no more worms or crawling bugs to swoop down on and pluck. All buried in cement, all killed by fertilizer and malnutrition, all driven away by automobiles. The last toad, for example, had died in 1970, and not gulped down by a falcon but run over by a truck driver. By now, it seemed that the only thing left to ensure the survival of winged wildlife in the vast and industrious region of Lombardy were the gardens of FIBA. And Augustus the Second was starting to think rather seriously that his mission in the world was not so much making buttons out of bone and mother-of-pearl as it was saving birds. Something similar, though on a larger scale, had also been done by the biblical Noah.

Anyway, for reasons that are not all that hard to figure out, he was not in a position to neglect the factory altogether, and in fact, as has been said, once or twice a day he stopped into Administration, received from the trembling hands of Signorina Rosa papers to sign, signed them, and went immediately back out to the gardens, where on occasion he was joined, in search of instructions or clarifications, by bookkeeper Cusetti or foreman Radice, to whom Augustus the Second invariably replied that everything must be done as it had been done in the time of his grandfather Augustus, bless his soul.

One day, Palmira Radice came to see him in the gardens, with a box of buttons in hand, to suggest a new, more rational way of packing them. To her, too, he replied standoffishly that everything must continue as it had been conceived by his blessed grandfather. Then, when she turned to go, in truth a bit downhearted, he gave her a quick pat on the fanny, a touch that was delicate but at the same time firm, and she twisted her head around, a bit dismayed, or perhaps more amazed actually, but all things considered without rebuff. Indeed, with no rebuff at all.

Later that evening, at twilight, when the antiquated machines of FIBA had finally quieted down and Augustus the Second, having looked after the daytime birds, was getting ready to turn his attention to the nocturnal ones, they too afflicted by industrialization, Palmira reappeared in the gardens, saying she had stayed on after hours in order to convince herself that the ideas of Augustus the Founder with regard to the packing of buttons were effectively better than the ideas that anyone who came after him might have on the question, and she had indeed convinced herself, but not without some fatigue, seeing as on that day she had not been able to avail herself of all her faculties because the caress that the boss had given her on a part of herself that she too was particularly fond of had put fire in her veins and left a void in her brain.

"But I didn't do it on purpose. I swear I didn't do it on purpose," Augustus the Second muttered, gasping for breath.

"Oh yes, you did!" she exclaimed, resolute, and she grabbed him, pulled him to her, and started running her hands and fingers over the most remote and sensitive parts of his body.

Augustus the Second was, in the most common sense of the word, a male. Although, because of his natural timidity, it had never happened to him, in the course of his by now thirty-four years of life to, so to speak, enjoy a woman. Now he felt very embarrassed, not for a defect in sexual potency, of which he was even oversupplied, but for uncertainty as to how to behave. In other words, he felt and understood that he should do something, but he didn't know what. "I," he finally muttered, "I, would really . . . But I've no experience; I don't know what to do. It's my first time . . ."

"So what?" Palmira cut him off, red hot. "I'm a virgin, too. But when two people love each other, they mustn't be afraid."

"Not here," Augustus the Second begged her. "Here, the birds can see us."

"You really think they care? They do it, too, you know," Palmira shot back.

"Yes, but only rarely do they let themselves be seen. They deserve some respect."

Palmira didn't lose her spunk. There was a shed nearby where gardening tools were kept as well as, luckily, cut grass, and right there, on the slightly seasoned cut grass, or better on a pile of smelly hay, she dragged him in and threw him down, and one thing led to another and before he knew it, she had offered up her virginity to him, although, when it comes to virginity, it's not always that easy to say.

Anyway, the thing was not at all unpleasant for Augustus the Second, and besides that, it was only the first round of amorous romping, night in and night out, ever more perfect and satisfying. Augustus the Second began to understand that besides loving birds, he could also love females. And the lovely Palmira, who even managed to say, at just the right time, the most socially convenient phrases, such as "Come here, my strong, handsome boss, my young husky master," was decidedly a female. And Augustus the Second began to appreciate, above and beyond her bonny backside, which had won him over at first sight, her breasts, her tummy, her thighs, and all of her accessible cavities.

And so a month went by, if not more. Most happily, to be sure. Then one day, while Augustus the Second was intent on feeding some migrating quail who were in great need of care, he was approached by Romeo Radice, the foreman.

Since the migrating quail, unaccustomed to the local environment, could easily be frightened, Augustus the Second motioned to him to stop and asked him, "What is it? One of the machines stop working?"

"No," the foreman replied decorously. "It's that my sister is pregnant."

Augustus the Second didn't stop tending to the quail, but he also pondered the news. Finally, he responded, "Fine. I'll do my duty as a gentleman. But for now, get the hell out of here."

The foreman Romeo Radice got the hell out of there, and that same night Augustus the Second confronted his mother.

His mother, Signora Belinda, had undergone an extraordinary change. Opposed so intrepidly by her son on that first day, she had immediately crumbled like a boxer hit by a thunderous uppercut, resigning herself to knitting and crocheting and to the profession of widow. She had good reason, in fact, to pine for her deceased husband, who had always suffered her abuse without saying incredible things like "Don't break my balls." Time and again during the day, she would mutter, "Giuseppe," and let out a sigh. She would gladly have brought him back to life. But that wasn't possible and it saddened her. Nevertheless, she had a reflux of vivacity when her son Augustus the Second informed her that he was going to marry Signorina Palmira Radice from the packing and shipping department. "You're out of your mind," she declared.

"I'm not out of my mind," he replied meekly.

"You're a Valle," she said, and she started weeping but without much conviction. Then she added, "Remember the last words of your poor father."

But Augustus the Second said, "I don't give a damn about the last words of my poor father."

And she said, "Marry her, but I'll die."

Chapter the Fourth

In which, as Signora Palmira
is left rather frustrated,
another character leaves us.

It was a curious wedding. That the bride, despite everything, would go to the altar dressed in white and, what's more, with her train held by two page boys, was what everybody expected, but nobody could ever have imagined that Augustus the Second would present himself in a morning suit that fit him to a tee.

At the factory, where work had not been suspended, the thing was the subject of some rather harsh comments, albeit sotto voce. The proletarians couldn't see why the boss should spend so much money to marry a whore. This shop floor commentary was going on at the same time as the ceremony, taking full advantage of the circumstance that the foreman, Romeo Radice, was about to become the boss's brother-in-law, for which reason he was in church, a partici-pant in the event.

The news that the boss had donned a morning suit for his wedding also penetrated the Administration. Bookkeeper Cusetti smirked discreetly, but Signorina Rosa blanched, and then blushed, and then, citing the usual disturbance of her bowels, got up to go to the toilet. But instead, she raced, so to speak, to the church.

There was a fair-sized crowd, largely made up of relatives of the bride, dressed in their ceremonial best, determined to show everyone what a leap in social status they were making. Signorina Rosa made her way into the crowd, pushing for-ward but a little to one side, and when she finally caught a glimpse of the bride and groom kneeling together at the altar, she nearly exploded in a scream. The morning suit, in fact, as evidenced by the odor of mothballs, was the morning suit of Augustus the Founder, and Augustus the Second had re-exhumed it for the occasion from some secret wardrobe.

The old woman's mind was then flooded by a rapid suc-cession of hallucinations, whereby, in a confused superim-position of time and circumstance, Augustus the Second turned into Augustus the First, and when the officiating priest asked Signorina Palmira, in accordance with the lit-urgy and the law, if she wished to take as her lawfully wed-ded husband there present et cetera, et cetera, poor Signorina Rosa answered, "Yes," not in a whisper but right out loud so that everyone turned around to look at her, even the bride, and that was truly the only cheerful note in a wedding that was otherwise, all things considered, grim.

After the ceremony, Augustus the Second went home to doff the morning suit and get his suitcase. He knocked on the door of the bedroom in which his mother, suffering from some obscure malady, had been shut for ten days, from the moment, that is, when she decided to die in response to her son's wedding. As always, there was no answer to his knock. But anyway, he said to her through the closed door, "It all went fine," and it wasn't clear just what sentiment had pushed him to say that.

He waited a second to hear if by chance some answer would come and then added, "I'm leaving, and I'll be gone ten days. Don't go to the factory. Signorina Rosa is there to take care of everything."

This time, he didn't even wait for the answer that wouldn't be coming, and he left.

He left, as is only natural, for his wedding journey. To his bride he had said that for their honeymoon, they would be going to the city of the saint, and she had asked him if by chance he was referring to Padua, the city of Saint Anthony, which she had never seen but which she also didn't have much desire to see, and he had replied that it wasn't Padua, and so she, a bit audaciously, had thought of San Remo, where at that very time they would be holding the song festival that ever since she was a little girl she had watched on TV, all three nights, before some obscure oversight committee had imposed on an entire country to do without two of the three. There, she thought, her strange and in many ways entrancing husband, by taking her to San Remo for the festival, was defying the arrogant callousness of people who, their own hearts having hardened, wanted everyone else's to harden, too. Fascists, Palmira considered them, even though now, by matrimony and wealth, she was no longer a proletarian.

But instead of San Remo, the city of the popular songs, Signora Palmira came to find herself in the city of Saint Francis of the downtrodden, or rather Assisi, where, shit, there was a festival of sacred music going on.

However, it wasn't for the sacred music that Augustus the Second had made the long journey to a place that was, all in all, out of the way, nor for the olive trees that "made the slopes pallid and smiling with sanctity," nor for the clear sky and breathable air. He had dragged himself all the way there for the sole purpose of admiring, in person and up close, the famous painting by Giotto whose photographic reproduction he had hung in Administration on the wall opposite his desk.

Indeed, upon their arrival in the town perched so sweetly on its hills, Augustus the Second, even before going to drop their bags at the "Sister Moon" pension, where he had reserved a double room with bath, raced off, holding his recent bride by the hand, to steal into the upper basilica, where he effortlessly discovered his painting. Nobody had ever told him so, but he knew that it was right there, where, indeed, it was.

He stood before it, immediately fascinated but then also a bit amazed and bewildered, not so much because of the extraordinary nature of the deed represented, for to him there was nothing extraordinary about it, but rather because, voilà!, through the art of a consummate painter, something so fundamentally normal as chatting with a few songbirds was portrayed as sacred, or even miraculous, and in the end he felt, not without trepidation, caught up in the sacredness. And as this sort of spiritual uplift pervaded him, he kept on holding his recent bride by the hand, maybe out of distraction or maybe because unconsciously he was hoping that even she, perhaps helped in some way by the flux of emotion that he himself was undoubtedly emanating, would rise to the sphere of superior perception and supernatural relation that we customarily call mysticism. But Signora Palmira, on account of her nature and constitution, was not cut out for such celestial journeys, and anyway, the thing couldn't even get off the ground due to the intervention of a humble

Franciscan friar who came to say, so what if the lady was dressed in a way that was a bit too revealing; so what if, instead of praying, she was constantly working her chewing gum; but the transistor radio crackling with the dear songs of that profane festival had better be turned off.

"If that's the way it is, we'll go outside," replied Palmira, full of decorum, and she put the accent on "we" so the little friar would understand that she would also be depriving the cult of Saint Francis of her husband who, if he had married her without putting up a fight, must be the kind of jerk who did everything other people wanted him to do.

But her husband, without taking his eyes off of the sacred painting, replied, "You go outside, and don't break my balls."

Signora Palmira looked at him, at first incredulous but then very quickly indignant, hating him more than she had hated him up to that moment because she could see perfectly well that the jerk would not be moved. So she stiffened her back and, still working her gum and listening to the radio, went out to the square in front of the church where, little by little, her anger waning but her self-pity waxing, she began to think that their marriage, which she had firmly desired, not to say plotted for, might actually be a calamity if the man she married, instead of taking her to the San Remo festival, had brought her to this place for losers that made her feel so melancholy.

Eight days they stayed in Assisi, and she never again set foot in the basilica, where that friar had treated her so discourteously. She stayed in bed with her trusty radio and her thoughts, or, still listening to the radio but with fewer bad thoughts, she went to sit in the sun at a table in some outdoor café.

He, on the other hand, outfitted with a hunting stool he had bought for himself, spent the whole day, until the light grew too dim, sitting in front of his fresco. He seemed a dullard but was actually searching, although confusedly and all in all without a lot of torment, for a more uplifting justification for having found himself in the world talking to birds. Who knows, maybe he would have managed to find that more uplifting justification, or rather, in plain words, he might at least have gotten closer to his own state of holiness, but for the fact that in him, as in any other being but in a form certainly more exalted and distinct, there was both good and evil, the wolf and the little boy, so that after all that daytime uplift, when darkness fell, in a sort of schizophrenic dichotomy, he was overcome with lust and wantonness. So in the double room with bath at the pension "Sister Moon," he threw himself like a madman on the body of his bride.

He relished that body to the point of delirium, not only its perfectly modeled buttocks but also everything about it that was soft and curvaceous. And there was plenty to relish. Abundant, firm breasts, round tummy, raised pubic mound, glorious hips, shoulders and arms and feet. He gazed at it, caressed it, kissed it, licked it, all the while emitting sounds of sensual gratification.

The bride, gum in her mouth and radio at her ear, let him do as he wished. Only sometimes, when it seemed to her that he was dragging things out a little too much, she would intervene to ask, "But when are we going back home? We can't spend all this time away from the factory!"

"Signorina Rosa will look after the factory," he answered, still grazing.

And she took offense. "She's deaf, blind, old, and brainless. What do you mean she'll look after the factory?"

"She'll look after it. She knows how things were done in my grandfather's time, bless his soul."

Signora Palmira would have liked to tell him exactly what she thought about his blessed grandfather and his entire family of nutcases, but she held back, waiting for a more opportune time. She felt, how to put it, as though she were expanding.

Anyway, the time eventually came for them to head home.

As soon as they arrived, Augustus the Second went to the door of the bedroom where his mother had shut herself in and said, "I'm back, Mama. Everything went fine."

He obviously got no response.

Signora Belinda, as everyone knew by now, was not doing well at all. A few days earlier, her personal physician, Doctor Bardi, had come to examine her and he was worried. Unable to come up with a diagnosis, he had advised hospitalization, but the patient had said no and had refused to allow the doctor to examine her again. So her personal physician was kept outside the door, too, asking her questions that never got an answer: Had she had a bowel movement? Did she have a fever? Feel pain, nausea, dizziness? Nothing.

A few days later, however, she sent for her son. She didn't even look at him. She waited for him to come to her bedside and said to him, "You're the one who wanted me to die."

Augustus the Second did not comment.

After a long pause, Signora Belinda added, "Your father was a half-wit, you're a total nitwit, and your wife is a whore."

Even then, Augustus the Second made no comment.

Signora Belinda let an even longer silence go by, summoned her energies, and concluded, "The child that will be born is not yours. The father is Carlo Vigeva. And now, get out of here. Let me die in peace."

She died during the night without any further disturbance.

Chapter the Fifth

In which, though not exactly longed for,
a little boy arrives on the scene.

The funeral of Signora Belinda Sassi offered the entire Radice clan the occasion for a new, sensational move upward on their climb toward bourgeois status. They were all there, all wearing with evident melancholy the same outfits they had worn with equally evident gaiety at the wedding just a few days earlier, except, naturally for her, Signorina Palmira Radice now Signora Palmira Valle, who was decked out in a stunning mourning dress, skintight, which in everybody's opinion made her look like a movie star. The most luxuriant wreath of flowers was, needless to say, hers, as demonstrated beyond the shadow of a doubt by the words in large gold letters on the accompanying black ribbon: "Her Inconsolable Daughter-in-Law—Palmira Radice Valle." With no chewing gum in her mouth and no radio to her ear, she played her inconsolable role with surprising aplomb, squeezing out huge quantities of tears into a lovely, embroidered handkerchief.

But later, re-entering the house from the cemetery, in the very act of removing from her comely head her long black veil, she said firmly, "Now it's me who's in command here."

"You're not in command of a damn thing," Augustus the Second answered her equally firmly. "And if you dare set foot in the factory, you're going right back to the packing department, which is where you belong."

"If you think you're going to make me croak like you made your mother croak, you're making a big mistake," Signora Palmira rebutted unabashed. "I was born poor and I'm not one of the gentle folk. But remember, I've got your child in my belly."

"Mine, or Carlo Vigeva's?" Augustus the Second asked brusquely, staring straight at her.

At first, Signora Palmira looked as if she hadn't understood the question, then she looked stupefied, and finally she opted for a sort of disdain but quite contained. "Who told you that?" she asked flatly.

"So they say," Augustus the Second shot back laconically.

Signora Palmira remained suspended for a minute and then exploded. "It was that whore of a mother of yours who planted the doubt in your head. Fine, hold on to it. But then what difference does it make if it's yours or Vigeva's? Either way, he'll have your name. And he'll inherit your money."

Augustus the Second shrugged. "But you, don't you set foot in the factory," he said, and he walked off to the gardens and his birds. He confided in them that he was not very happy about the way things were going.

A few months went by with no big news. Just that Signora Palmira's belly was getting bigger and bigger, as was inevitable. She was very agitated and couldn't wait to rid herself of that load. She even confessed as much to bookkeeper Cusetti, who one hot day came to ask her for a glass of cold water. She gave him a Coca-Cola. And she said to him, "When I was Signorina Palmira of the packing and shipping department, I really liked you, but I didn't have the courage to tell you because I was a factory hand and you were the bookkeeper."

"And now maybe you don't like me anymore," the bookkeeper sighed.

"Now . . ." Palmira said, patting her belly. "Look at what bad shape I'm in. Feel them, feel my hips. I look like a cow."

"You drive me crazy even like this," said the bookkeeper, feeling her here and there.

Signora Palmira was flattered, but in the end her proletarian savvy prevailed and she didn't give in. "Wait till I unload the kid," she said, "and then you'll see."

She delivered on September 14, in the Roses Clinic, a concrete block surrounded by other concrete blocks. As for the roses, nobody could remember seeing them around there, but the name boded well.

Augustus the Second did what expectant fathers commonly do in such circumstances—namely, he paced up and down in the hallway while Signora Palmira was in the delivery room, but he gave the impression that he was doing it by imitation rather than out of real anxiety. Nobody, on looking at him, would have been able to tell if what was happening made him happy or not. Actually, it didn't make him happy at all, given that he thought the child belonged to Carlo Vigeva, a childhood friend he hadn't seen in years, mostly because the guy was totally absorbed in making wheelbarrows. He tried to convince himself that a child was really not all that different from a bird with regard to which there is no interest at all in knowing who its father is, the important thing being that it's alive and well. But he just couldn't manage—not even with the help of Saint Francis—to become so charitable. He couldn't bring himself to feel any love for the baby. He wouldn't give a damn if it were born dead.

But he was born alive and he was very beautiful, for a baby, and Signora Palmira looked radiant with joy. "Now go to the registry of births and register his name as Patrizio," she told her husband.

"He'll have my surname and I'll give him the name I want," replied Augustus the Second.

"I gave birth to him and you'll call him Patrizio," Signora Palmira confirmed.

Augustus the Second went to the registry of births and reported that a male child had been born to him at such and such a place and time and said that he wanted to call him Giuseppe.

"Christ," said the man at the registry, who was a friend of his, "but that's the name of your father who jumped off the bell tower."

"We'll see if this one jumps, too," Augustus the Second replied gravely.

Chapter the Sixth

In which, because of his hatred for plastic,
and his love for ecology,
the life of Augustus the Second
enters yet more dire straits.

Thrush and redwing, blackbirds and finches, ravens and star-lings, bunting, skylarks, wagtails and pipits, tree-creepers and Bohemian waxwings, grackles and magpies, titmice and shrike, flycatchers, whitethroats, swallows and wrens and alpine accen-tors, wheatear and robins, all passerines and sprightly singers of songs, continued to gladden the days of Augustus the Second. His nights, on the other hand, were gladdened by his spouse, or better, by her body, since she, understood as a sentient and rea-soning entity, did not participate in her husband's banquets of the senses. "You're a lurid, disgusting pig," she sometimes said to him.

"Yes, yes," he answered, happy as could be.

"If you don't stop I'm going to vomit."

"Yes, yes." In his masochistic fervor, it seemed to him that everything was going just fine.

And she took offense. She denied him her breast, or her tummy, or some other part of herself that in that moment was exciting his oral cupidity.

"Let me go on," he implored her.

And she: "Why don't you put the factory in my name?" Or, "Why don't you appoint my brother as vice president?"

"Never."

"We'll see. He who endures conquers."

"I'll be the one who endures."

She never granted him a mutual orgasm. For better or worse, however, he got to where he wanted to go, then he slid over to his side of the bed and, falling back effortlessly into his little boy self, drifted off to sleep listening to hoopoes and owls and, naturally, to sublime nightingales.

She, who slept during the day, had trouble getting to sleep at night, and since she took no pleasure in birdsongs, she kept her mind occupied with hate. But she was also prone to fear of God and she prayed to the Lord not to induce her into the temptation of killing her husband.

By way of compensation, however, she cheated on him, with her personal physician Doctor Colbiati, and with the mayor, attorney Matiussi, and not only because she thought it wise to keep those powerful men on her side but because she instinctively felt that that was another way to elevate her position on the social scale. Bookkeeper Cusetti, meanwhile, she kept on the back burner. She never lost a chance, with sultry looks and moves, to make him fall even harder for her, but she gave him nothing, or almost nothing, convinced that it was a good way to stimulate his efficiency.

And indeed it worked. What she wanted from him was not only a detailed account of what went on in Administration but also a plan for the expansion of the factory and constant psychological pressure on the boss as a complement to the pressure that she herself applied in other settings since that fathead wouldn't let her set foot in the factory.

For his part, bookkeeper Cusetti was utterly convinced that it was a fool's errand to keep on making buttons out of bone and mother-of-pearl, as in the nineteenth century, when in this day and age plastic was everywhere. "Plastic buttons, that's where the money is," he told the boss.

"No plastic. Humanity is going to die buried under a mountain of plastic," Augustus the Second declared.

"So then," Cusetti cleverly insisted, "why don't we change our whole operation? Anything would earn more than buttons, even wheelbarrows. Look at Carlo Vigeva . . ."

Carlo Vigeva was the one name the boss could not abide. "Nobody dare mention that name around here!" he shouted and furiously rushed out to the gardens to console himself with the passerines.

"Utterly mad!" Cusetti commented, honestly unable to understand the reason for such fury because Signora Palmira hadn't let him in on all her secrets.

"You're the one who's mad!" Signorina Rosa scolded him. "A man who respects tradition and venerates his grandfather is not mad but wise."

"I bet he finds money revolting."

"Because he obeys the Lord's commandments."

Bookkeeper Cusetti hadn't the least desire to get involved in a theological debate with that bubbleheaded old lady and he went into the kitchen to Signora Palmira to ask her for a glass of cold water. "He'll never give in," he said, devouring her with his eyes.

"He'll give in all right," she replied, more out of anger than conviction. She didn't leave any openings, however, for the desires of the bookkeeper, who, his glass now empty, sighed and headed for the door. That woman drove him wild, and he would gladly have thrown himself into the fire for her, but he would even more gladly have thrown himself on top of her to make love, and his heart told him that it would happen, but when, when?

But when, but when was what Signora Palmira was asking herself as well, as she went over to the window to watch her husband talking to the birds. He was harmless, everybody said, but he was harming her. And that child, who rather than Patrizio was named Giuseppe, was crying in the other room, and she couldn't bring herself to love him much, him having been the cause and the instrument of that marriage that had given her such little satisfaction up to now. Anyway, she was going to keep fighting until she won.

One night at bedtime, she was sitting on the side of the bed and Augustus the Second, already overcome with lust and kneeling in front of her, was taking off her shoes. She chewed her gum in meditation. After her shoes, he took off her stockings and started kissing her feet ravenously.

"I cheated on you today," she announced.

"Oh yeah?" he said without letting himself be distracted.

"I betrayed you with the mayor," she specified.

This time, he didn't even utter the laconic oh yeah, and she took offense. "Stop licking my feet. Besides, they're dirty. Listen to me," she said sharply.

Reluctantly, he took his lips off her feet and tilted his head to listen.

"I don't like getting fucked by the mayor," she said.

"Why did you do it?"

"For you," she declared. "You don't deserve it, but I did it for you."

"Thank you," he said, and she took offense again.

"Who do you think you are?" she shouted. "Sure, you're the owner of the factory, but I don't work there anymore. I'm an owner, too." She calmed down a little and continued. "I went to bed with the mayor because if I didn't, the Christian Democrats would have expropriated your gardens. They were going to approve an amendment to the zoning plan and turn them into a public park.

"The mayor is a Christian Democrat, too," Augustus the Second pointed out.

"But in order to have me, he voted with the opposition, and now the gardens are an industrial zone." Signora Palmira seemed very happy about that and finished her thought like this: "Industrial zone means it's worth millions. Since it's all thanks to me, now I'm the one who decides what to do with it."

"What to do with it?" asked Augustus the Second flabbergasted.

"Don't ask me questions with that dumb look on your face," she reprimanded him. "There are two alternatives: either sell the gardens and use the money to renovate the factory to make plastic buttons, plastic belt buckles, maybe even plastic tubs, like Montedison . . ."

"That I'll never do!" Augustus the Second couldn't contain himself from screaming.

"Or," she went on, paying no heed to the interruption, even though it had annoyed her, "or we sell the gardens and use the money to buy an apartment in a skyscraper in Piazza della Repubblica in Milan, and we move there to live the life of the upper crust."

"I'll never do that either," Augustus the Second said.

He said it firmly but not aggressively, and he was already calmly preparing to go back to kissing her feet, but this time, she wouldn't have it. "The gardens are yours and you won't sell them. But my body is mine and for you it's now off limits. I'm not going to let you touch me ever again, not even a finger."

She, too, had spoken firmly but not aggressively, and Augustus the Second realized that he was coming to the end of one phase of his life and was about to begin another in which his birds would be his only consolation. Without objection, he took his pillow and a blanket that was on the bed and he started off, with a bearing that was certainly more decorous than might be expected, toward the adjacent room.

The adjacent room was the bedroom of little Giuseppe who, on his father's entrance, woke up and started crying. Augustus the Second did not change his demeanor. He walked over to a couch bed, arranged his pillow and blanket on it, and lay down, pulling the blanket up over his head, pretending not to hear the baby's crying, or at least not to feel any responsibility for it, seeing as he wasn't the one who had brought him into the world.

Chapter the Seventh

In which Augustus the Second,
after making it understood that he
wants no innovations,
glimmers just a little, with sanctity.

Augustus the Second endured it, but enduring it was dire, and the direst part was the loneliness that came with it, since, with the exception of Signorina Rosa in Administration and the birds in the gardens, there, all around him, everyone was against him.

In truth, little Giuseppe, who was not yet able to make distinctions between actual father and putative father, was quite well disposed toward him, whom he considered his true and only father, and he smiled at him, kicking his legs, and holding his arms out as if to hug him, or at least to touch him, but Augustus was hard. "Stop right there!" he would say to him gruffly. "Do you think I can enter into confidence with Vigeva's boy?" And he went off to talk with the birds or to the factory, where he had found ways to make himself useful, or at least to do something.

He had, in fact, bought an enormous quantity of prints picturing birds of all kinds and colors, even exotic ones, and he made the frames for them himself in a corner of the polishing department. One by one, as he framed the prints, he hung them on the walls, not only in Administration but also in the various departments of the factory itself.

The men and women factory hands grumbled, saying that this was the boss's way of taunting them, but it was a good bet that they were not expressing their own opinions but rather the opinion of the foreman, Romeo Radice, who, having realized that he was never going to become vice president, was irritated by having the boss under foot there in the factory, making frames and hanging pictures. "Why doesn't he worry about the factory instead of the birds?" he went around saying to the workers. "He could be giving work to a hundred people instead of thirty. But if we stay united and determined, one day or another we'll hit him with a strike that he'll never forget."

Augustus the Second knew about all this, or at least he imagined it, but it didn't bother him at all. On the contrary, he hung more and more pictures of birds on the wall just to spite the foreman. And when he was finished there, he carried on in Administration, to spite bookkeeper Cusetti.

Bookkeeper Cusetti, most assuredly obeying the orders of Signora Palmira, never tired of proposing new plans to him: modernize here and modernize there, knock down this and rebuild that. "My grandfather, bless his soul, wouldn't like that," Augustus the Second responded invariably.

And after a while, the bookkeeper, in further evidence that he was not acting on his own but on behalf of Signora

Palmira, whom he coveted more and more, would make yet another proposal.

And one day, while Cusetti, all absorbed in charts and figures, was busy trying to illustrate the advantages of a grandiose American machine that cost seven hundred million lire because it churned out buttons one after another at an incredible pace, almost as though it were printing thousand lire notes, Augustus the Second, miffed, swiftly opened his desk drawer, pulled out a fake mustache identical to his grandfather's, and stuck it to his upper lip.

When she saw him, Signorina Rosa let out a scream and fainted. Cusetti let out a scream, too, and understood once and for all that the boss was never going to innovate.

Meanwhile, Augustus the Second rushed to the aid of poor Signorina Rosa, and thanks to repeated slaps on the face, managed to bring her around, but he had forgotten the fake mustache under his nose, and Signorina Rosa, on seeing it right in front of her eyes, was convinced that she had crossed over into the other world, and she fainted again.

So Augustus the Second took off the mustache, brought her around a second time, and then went out to the gardens to report to the birds.

Bookkeeper Cusetti, meanwhile, went to report to Signora Palmira. "I can't take it anymore," he confessed. "Fire me, if you want, don't let me even get near you, but I just can't deal with your husband anymore."

"Don't you abandon me now, too, Armando," she said to him, taking him by the hand. "You're the only smile in these sad gray days of mine."

Cusetti's heart was beating so fast that he couldn't get a word out of his mouth.

They were standing in front of the window overlooking the gardens, and right in front of their eyes was Augustus the

Second, so covered with birds he looked like a German tourist in Saint Mark's Square. "I hate him, I hate him," Signora Palmira muttered grimly with a look on her face worthy of Lady Macbeth. Indeed, she went on, "Oh, if only he would die! If only he would drop dead right now!" And then, finally, "Armando, you wouldn't kill him for my love, would you?"

Bookkeeper Cusetti was certainly young and enamored, but he was also a little too delicate to take on a responsibility like the one his lady love was proposing. "Kill him," he said as though he were entertaining the idea. "If you ask me, that guy deserves something worse than death. I mean, for example, why don't you have him declared incompetent?"

"Right, declare him incompetent, it should be that simple," Signora Palmira observed with a tone of disappointment tinged with bitterness. "You don't think I've considered that? There would have to be some precedents, some supporting witnesses." Then, resigned, she concluded hastily, "All I can do is put horns on his head. Come on, let's go."

She really didn't want to waste time. She was already dragging him behind her, toward the master bedroom and the nuptial bed.

Bookkeeper Cusetti had been dreaming of a moment like this. He had been fantasizing about it for so long that seeing it unfolding before him in the here and now paralyzed him with emotion, not to mention that deep down, he also had the suspicion that her sudden decision was a cover-up for some trick to force him into committing that murderous violence from which he, for his part, was backing away. "Right here, in his own bed?" he said half-lost. "And if he walks in and finds us here?"

"I wish," Signora Palmira shot back briskly, and she didn't bother explaining what there might be behind that "I wish." Without a lot of preliminaries, she made him comfortable on the bed and then started unbuttoning his shirt and pants, seemingly in a frenzy. "Finally, a man," she said breathlessly. "And young and distinguished, finally."

The more of him she uncovered, the more Cusetti appealed to her. "Finally," she said again and started kissing him lasciviously all over his body, all the while saying to him in snippets, "It's been months now that I haven't let that pig touch me. You know what he did to me, that scumbag? He didn't just fuck me like a man, you know. He would kiss me, lick me all over. I was nothing more than an instrument of his base pleasure. . . ."

In that moment, Augustus the Second was telling the birds that men had turned sex into a baneful artificial construct, a way of doing harm to self and others, and he himself had gotten lost for a time in that dark wood, but now, thank heaven, he was fairly able to sublimate his desires and he no longer suffered, neither abstinence nor betrayal. He spoke with a sweet voice, and the expression on his face was seraphic, and as he spoke, a light took shape on his head, perhaps in the form of a halo, and probably it was just a matter of rays of sunlight filtering through the leaves on the trees, but in any case, it was light.

Chapter the Eighth

*In which, finally, nearly everyone goes
on strike, while also a little boy
comes to an understanding with the birds.*

The big strike hoped for by foreman Romeo Radice was given a way to break out when the owner of FIBA personally affixed to the bulletin board of the Factory Council a letter on the official stationery of "Italia Nostra" in which the president of the beneficent association—the writer Giorgio Bassani—appropriately thanked Mr. Augustus the Second Valle who had sent him a voluntary contribution of three million lire in support of the campaign then being conducted by Italia Nostra against fowling.

Immediately a strike committee was formed, captained, naturally, by Romeo Radice, who, accompanied by three delegates, paid a visit to Administration in order to confront the owner. "You're my brother-in-law," he said to him, "but you are also the boss, and before you the boss, I am a proletarian among proletarians and I speak also in the name of all the workers of FIBA, men and women."

"Speak," Augustus the Second said to him a bit too regally.

"By affixing that letter to our bulletin board," Romeo Radice began, "you committed both an illegality and a provocation. Illegality because the bulletin board is ours, it belongs to the Factory Council, and you, if you want to post a notice, you can go post it in the toilet. Provocation because no one throws away three million lire on fowling."

"To oppose fowling," Augustus the Second corrected him.

"Ah, go on, you understood me perfectly; a word to the wise is sufficient."

"And my words will be very few," said Augustus the Second. "It's my money and I do what I want with it."

"Once upon a time, in your grandfather's time, maybe that's the way it was. But now . . ."

Augustus the Second cut him off. "To me, it's always by grandfather's time," he declared, and to give more weight to his declaration, he opened his desk drawer quick as a wink, pulled out his trusty fake mustache, and stuck it under his nose.

That meant strike, naturally, and the cacophonous machines went silent, and in the entire plant, Administration included, only Signorina Rosa remained at her post.

"Why don't you leave, too?" Augustus the Second asked her. As always, it was hard to tell if the strike displeased him or not.

"Leave me here, Signor Augustus," Signorina Rosa implored him. "They might hurt you."

Augustus the Second couldn't understand how they could hurt him. Nevertheless, he let her stay where she wished, and since it was dinnertime, he went over to his residence, to the kitchen, where he usually took his meals.

In the kitchen, he found the stove unlit, the table not set, little Giuseppe running around crying that he was hungry, and his wife, Palmira, disdainfully sitting apart, away from the table. "Aren't we eating today?" he asked humbly.

"I'm on strike, too," Signora Palmira proclaimed. "In this house I'm nothing more than an exploited proletarian. Not to mention that with the three million lire you could have bought me a mink coat worthy of a factory owner's wife."

Augustus the Second had no objections. He looked in the refrigerator. There were eggs and cheese. He took out a piece of cheese. Then he took a piece of bread, too. He was about to leave when he sensed the inquisitive gaze of the little boy named Giuseppe Valle staring at him. He stood there as though in doubt about whether to pay attention to him or not, thinking as always that after all, he was not his son. Then he resolved to give him a piece of bread anyway along with a piece of cheese.

He also gave some bread crumbs and cheese crumbs to the passerines that came flying to greet him when he appeared in the gardens.

"Cheep, cheep, cheep," they sang to thank him.

And he spoke to them, saying that civilization was beginning to break his balls and that an idea was spinning around in his head that had fascinated him ever since he was a kid, which was the idea of becoming a monk.

As he was making this speech, the little boy Giuseppe was coming up behind him. He came walking forward without scaring the birds until he was side by side with his putative father, still unaware of him, and since his father was talking to the birds, he, too, started talking to the birds, saying, "Cheep, cheep, cheep," and the birds, all happy, answered, "Cheep, cheep, cheep," and flew all around him, perched on his shoulders and on top of his head, and a little at a time, even though it was a foggy day, a halo of light took shape around his blond hair.

Then, all of a sudden, Augustus the Second saw him and he couldn't believe his eyes. But he convinced himself that he wasn't seeing things, and so he forgot about the birds and knelt down in the mud before the boy, who was smiling at him.

"It just might be," he muttered, "it just might be that you're my son and not Vigeva's. Why couldn't you be my son?"

Then he started to cry and hugged him tight. And all of the birds were happy to see it.

Chapter the Ninth

*In which some things are clarified,
but others become more obscure.*

It was one of those heavy fog days, darkness at noon, and the big trucks on the roads around Milan, mostly trailer trucks, had their headlights on as they lumbered along, making the earth tremble and splattering everything with smog-soaked muck. And besides the trucks, there were swarms of impatient automobiles, and vans and minivans, and motorcycles, motorbikes, and motor scooters, and just one man riding a bicycle, wrapped up in an overcoat but bareheaded, his hair dripping from the smog and his face smudged with smog, and it was, needless to say, Augustus the Second. As usual, his face showed no anxiety or any other visible sentiment. He was pedaling along on the shoulder of the road so he wouldn't be run over by the traffic, making his way forward without worrying about the mud splashes, at a moderate but constant speed, giving the impression, all things considered, of strength, or at least of doggedness, like someone who has resolved to do something and is well determined to see it through to the end. He had, in fact, resolved to clarify once and for all the mystery of the paternity of his son, Giuseppe, and so he was going to see Vigeva, who had his workshop four or five kilometers from FIBA, and he was going there by bicycle because if the world was going to be saved from death by pollution, somebody had to start going from one place to another without emitting carbon dioxide.

Vigeva's workshop could be seen from a distance by way of a reddish glow, reminiscent of Dante's Malebolge, illuminating the gloomy fog. Drawing closer, it became evident that the glow was caused by an enormous neon sign mounted on top of the tallest of the factory buildings: "Vigeva Metalworks and Machine Shop." Augustus the Second pulled in there and they didn't make him wait because, after all, he too was an industrialist, a factory owner.

Carlo Vigeva, owner and chief executive of the machine shop by the same name, was a man of the same age as Augustus the Second but burly and also a little boorish and yet with an air of the grandiose about him, almost as though he were a relative of the god Vulcan, something that became more evident when he happened to be, as he was now, in the main building.

It was an enormous construction, blazing with bursts of lurid flames, pulsing with the incredible bedlam of the machines that were pouring out incandescent metal, or pounding out sheet metal with earsplitting mallet blows, or shooting nails, or triumphantly carrying around metallic skeletons that were gradually outfitted with parts and accessories until they became, at the end of the process, wheelbarrows. The wheelbarrows were in fact the objective of all this activity. The four high walls were inscribed, in big cubic letters, with a suggestive slogan coined by Carlo Vigeva himself: "Work: The world needs wheelbarrows."

He, the owner, was there in the middle of the uproar, and the smoke, and the glare, and he was working like the others, more than the others, rushing around tirelessly here and there, encouraging and inciting his men, with words and by example, even with profanity if necessary, and he didn't show the slightest sign of joy when he noticed Augustus the Second, who had come all the way there to look for him. "What do you want?" he asked him gruffly, shouting at the top of his lungs to be heard over the noise.

"I need to talk to you!" Augustus the Second shouted back.

"Speak! Don't waste my time!"

This invitation was discouraging, not only because of the need to shout but also because Vigeva, who never took his eyes off the production process, seemed ill-disposed to listen. "Not here; it's a delicate matter."

"Can't you come by on Sunday?"

"It's urgent!"

Vigeva would have gladly shouted back that he should go fuck himself, but he was, deep down, a sentimental type, and he and Augustus the Second had been friends once, even schoolmates. So he gestured to him to wait, went over to yell at some loafers who were sloughing off on the job, gave a hand to some others who were having trouble moving a crate, gave a kick to still another who was hiding in a corner to smoke a cigarette in peace, and then came back to his erstwhile friend and led him outside through a little side door, into the fog, blood red with neon. "So what is it you need to tell me that's so urgent?"

What he needed to tell him Augustus the Second had thoroughly prepared during his bicycle ride. Nevertheless, when he started into his little speech, it came out haltingly, convoluted, discontinuous, and all in all, not quite right for the place, not to mention his listener. "Paternity," he began by saying, "is not just a matter of biology . . . animal biology, so to speak . . . but it's also a matter of religion . . . of metaphysics . . . even the origin of our own Christian religion is all tied up with that question about the putative father. . . . Now, as I see it, but also according to the leaders of the church, what counts is metaphysical paternity. . . . Sure enough, biological paternity, it must be agreed, has its role. . . . We're not ready yet . . ."

Vigeva didn't let him go on. He grabbed him by the arm and shook him ferociously, saying to him, "Listen, they tell me you're not interested in making money, and that's your business. Everybody's got the right to break his balls however he wants. But money matters to me. I don't have time to waste with lunatics like you. Suppose you just tell me why you came looking for me?"

At this point, Augustus the Second, dejected, was visibly uncomfortable. Nevertheless, he got his courage up and asked the crucial question, "Who is Giuseppe's father?"

The question was crucial for him, not for Vigeva, who didn't know. "Giuseppe who?"

"Giuseppe, my son."

Vigeva was flabbergasted. "But if he's your son, what the hell are you looking for?"

Prodded, Augustus the Second turned feisty. "Are you trying to tell me you don't know how many cuckolds there are in this world?" he shot back vivaciously. "And bastard kids? And that you don't know what a whore my wife is? Ready and willing to be knocked up by you while she was engaged to me?"

Vigeva grabbed him by the neck as though he wanted to throttle him. "Listen to me carefully," he said. "I've never had anything to do with your wife. I'm an aristocrat, even if I've made my way up from the bottom. I don't like working-class women. They stink, you got that? And now, get the hell out of here. I wouldn't be surprised if your kid was fathered by a priest, but there is no way he's mine."

The more Vigeva squeezed his neck, the happier Augustus was. And not because he actually wanted to be strangled to death but because he saw in Vigeva's fury and facial expression something that was extremely coarse, and you could say anything about little Giuseppe except that he was coarse since in everything he said or did, he showed himself to be sweet and gentle, and anyone who was not sidetracked by malicious gossip could have established without any effort whatsoever who, between him and Vigeva, was the real father.

So he took his leave happily and, still laughing with happiness, headed back home on his bicycle, and up in the sky, above the blanket of smog, he could hear birds celebrating, and though he couldn't see them, he talked to them of the joy of having a son who was sweet and gentle, and he also talked about the misfortune of having a mother who was mean and scurrilous, and finally he would have liked to say something against his wife, Palmira, but he didn't feel up to it just then because until then, he had been thinking of her as more of a whore than she actually was.

And still laughing with happiness, despite being soaking wet and filthy with smog, he arrived home. The striking workers were all out in front of the factory, carrying signs that said bad things about him. But when somebody started to whistle at him in protest, somebody else shut him up, as though the boss had suddenly become worthy of respect and pity, filthy and bedraggled as he was. A little farther on, in front of the door to the house, there was an ambulance, which may have been connected to the strike in some way. At least that's what Augustus thought, and still unsuspecting, he went into the house.

But then he saw. There were two nurses, in the great entrance hall, and two carabinieri, and also a doctor, all waiting for him. Little Giuseppe was there, too, and, on seeing him come in, he would have liked to run up to him, but his mother was holding him back, as though trying to save him from some imminent danger. They were at the far end of the room, mother and son. Closer to the entrance was the doctor, who said, "Signor Valle, we're sorry, we have to take you away with us."

Augustus the Second still had a half smile on his face and he kept it in place, though it took a bit of effort. Then he moved, walking forward just slightly stiffly toward the little boy. He paid no attention at all to his wife, Palmira, who was saying, "We did it for your own good. . . . You'll come back home soon . . . cured . . ."

He looked only at the little boy. He stopped in front of him, held out his hand, and said to him, "Giuseppe, my son, take care of our birds. I have to go to the asylum."

"Yes, Papa," the boy replied.

Augustus the Second turned and walked back toward the door with his slightly stiff gait.

The nurses and carabinieri fell in on both sides to escort him.

Chapter the Tenth

In which Augustus the Second
resolves to go along.

So then, it was the asylum. But it wasn't terrible, at least not too terrible, considering the state of the world outside. There were the lunatics, to be sure, paranoids, fixated on being covered with fleas or convinced they could swim to the United States, schizophrenics with a split or even fragmented self but well-managed as they were, or rather kept under thumb by massive doses of psychotropic drugs, or by electroshock or insulin shock therapy, or even some combination of the above, they didn't cause a lot of trouble. Indeed, at a certain point, seen from the outside, even the most agitated among them didn't differ much from those who, because of their illness, were meek—that is, simply melancholic or depressed. Science, in other words, was good for something.

In the asylum there were also, obviously, women inmates who one met up with in the gardens during recreation, and they too were divided, who knows how empirically, into paranoids and schizophrenics, melancholics and manic depressives. Some of them, normally the ugliest and oldest, were convinced they were young and beautiful, and they decked themselves out extravagantly with colored ribbons and rags, painted their faces with outlandish makeup, and during the afternoon walk, as soon as they could do it without a nurse taking notice, they would, fast as lightning, walk up to a male inmate and ask under their breath, "Tell me, do you have a dick? Do you really? Show it to me." Or maybe, "Let me feel it." And some of the men, the really crazy ones, showed it to them or even let them touch it on the sly.

The first time he was approached that way by a madwoman who was really horrendous, Augustus the Second nearly ran away, but then, overcoming his disgust, he even smiled at her. "I, my lovely signorina, no longer have one. The rats ate it the other night." And she broke out laughing, with a crazed cackle, and then she started crying, but there was nothing he could do to console her.

Anyway, love opportunities aside, the recreation hour was very nice because there were five or six trees in the garden and a couple of flower beds with grass and flowers and, naturally, a few passerines, the sight of whom filled Augustus the Second with great joy but also with great sadness and regret because unfortunately, he had to stay away from them.

This special bit of prudence had been recommended to him by his lawyer whom he had called for legal advice. "I urge you," the old man had said to him, "no birds. For heaven's sake, don't get into relating to the birds here, too, or you'll never get out."

His wife, Palmira, the day she came to visit him, also told him he would never get out of there, not because of the passerines but for completely different reasons.

Doctor Caroniti, on the other hand, the friendly psychiatrist in whose hands he had happened into, had not intimated that the thing was going to be endless but that, yes, it would be rather long. This he had made him understand quite clearly. Not exactly because of the birds, however, with regard to which he had limited himself to observing that it was certainly an extravagance to dedicate himself to finches, which didn't yield any return, and not dedicate himself to buttons, which earned money. But he hadn't imposed any sort of prohibition, and in substance it appeared that he, if he wished to, could have brought into the asylum the entire community that was living out in the gardens and go back to conversing with them again without incurring any serious consequences. But why trust what some crazy people's doctor says? It might just be that the doctor wanted to demonstrate that Augustus hadn't overcome his old ornithological vice and by so doing, have an easy time of it not ever letting him out again. The asylum, as he was slowly but surely discovering, was a place where when somebody happened to end up inside, they tended to keep him in there as long as possible, even resorting to the artifice of declaring that insanity didn't exist so they could keep the sane people in there, too.

So the birds, rather than call them, it was better to beg them to stay away, to not come, and if during recreation one of them happened to come near him, he treated him, let's not say severely or brusquely, but he barely glanced at him out of the corner of his eye and spoke to him in a very low whisper, "You're Leopoldo, aren't you? I recognize you."

"Cheep, cheep, cheep," the other one answered, all smiles.

But Augustus the Second urged him, "Quiet, brother. Be on your way, for the love of God. Here, they'll get the better of me if they see that the two of us understand each other."

And the bird went on his way, singing, "Cheep, cheep, cheep," not like before but with sadness and compassion.

And one day, an inmate who had accidentally surprised him in conversation with a couple of ornery magpies who had come to perch on the lowest branch of one of those five trees, decided he was crazy.

It was wise, therefore, to resign himself, to adapt, or better to go along, as Doctor Caroniti had amicably suggested from their very first colloquy.

It had been a very nice exchange and, in the end, not completely discouraging, owing not so much to the merits of Augustus the Second as to the virtues of Doctor Caroniti who had a calm voice, sharp and cheery eyes behind his glasses, and an easy cordiality. "You see, Signor Valle," he had said right off the bat without a lot of hemming and hawing, "psychiatric illnesses are still rather mysterious. Don't pay attention to those who claim to know more about them than anyone else. . . ."

At that point, Augustus the Second, still new to the asylum, had made a small error—that is, he had responded by saying, "I don't pay attention to anyone, Doctor. I always think for myself."

Doctor Caroniti, consequently, must have had the impression that he was dealing with a truly crazy crazy person, one of those who maybe wasn't agitated but who would certainly be difficult to lead back to the straight and narrow. With great mastery, however, he had masked his feelings and gone ahead soothingly. "It's not easy, not even for experts, to establish whether someone is, or is not, mentally sane. Freud himself, the great master, was known to say that the border between normal psychic states and pathological ones is, on the one hand, purely conventional, and on the other, so fluid that each of us crosses it, in one direction or the other, several times a day, without even realizing it. Now, here I have a certificate from your personal physician . . . Doctor . . . Doctor . . ."

He stopped in mid-sentence, the able psychiatrist, as he delved through the numerous papers on his desk, looking for the certificate signed by Doctor . . . Doctor . . . , and Augustus the Second, only for the sake of saving him the bother of a search that threatened to be more than a little prolonged, committed a second small error by saying, "His name is Anacleto Colbiati, but he's not my doctor. He's my wife's doctor; he's been screwing her for at least two years now."

No matter how consummate the professional mastery a physician for the insane might possess, it's always possible that he'll be surprised, or even disconcerted, by something, especially if that something is full of common sense, as was, after all, Augustus the Second's comment. This observation, translated into doctrinal terms, means that when someone is suspected of insanity, the more he acts like a sane person the worse he makes matters for himself. But Augustus the Second didn't know this yet, and as for the psychiatrist, he managed once again to mask his discomposure quite well. "Ah yes, that's right, Doctor Colbiati," he had said with aplomb. "His certificate is right here." But then, realizing he had picked up the wrong document, he corrected himself. "No, this is the declaration of your wife, consenting to your commitment to a psychiatric institution . . ."

"Whore!" Augustus the Second could not contain himself from exclaiming, committing a third and much more serious error.

As often happens in the face of overly serious errors, Doctor Caroniti preferred, apparently, to ignore it, and he went ahead undaunted, "for as long as may be necessary, a declaration that, apart from everything else, we may consider superfluous. . . . Ah, here, finally is the certificate signed by Doctor Colbiati. . . ." He then read it in a low voice, swallowing some phrases and emphasizing others, and naturally only the latter could be understood by Augustus the Second: "state of psychomotorial excitement . . . requiring immediate hospitalization in a psychiatric institution . . . signed in three copies . . ." And having thus arrived at the end of the certificate, Doctor Caroniti, giving Augustus the Second a look that almost begged for confirmation, concluded, "So everything's in order."

How could Augustus the Second respond to that? They had set him up, that much was clear, and he had no choice but to go along with it. So he signaled his assent, albeit in the vaguest possible way, because deep down he still harbored a lot of doubts as to the regularity of the whole procedure.

Doctor Caroniti, in any event, felt reassured that he could proceed, and he quickly moved to what might be called the pragmatic part of his remarks. "Now," he said, "we are obliged by law to carry out some rather long, laborious, and anything but simple tests. We trust in your cooperation, above all for your own good."

They were words, it seemed to Augustus the Second, chosen purposely for dragging a person into a state of definitive prostration. "What must I do?" he asked with an exertion of goodwill.

"Nothing," the psychiatrist responded. "Nothing special. You must submit voluntarily to the examinations and tests, not interfere with the work of the hospital staff, maintain total confidence in our personnel who have been optimally trained. Basically, keep in mind that if you don't go along, there is always the agitated ward, where conditions are somewhat worse."

Augustus the Second, in all sincerity, didn't want things to be worse, but he didn't want to give in to blackmail either. "I am more than happy to oblige," he declared. "But if I've understood correctly, it's not up to you to prove I'm mad, but it's up to me to prove I'm sane. A difficult task for anyone. Try to imagine for a minute how it would be if the two of us were to change places."

This time, Doctor Caroniti couldn't quite bring himself to shrink from responding a little harshly. "First of all," he said, "try to avoid using terms like 'mad' and 'sane,' which don't exist for us. I thought I had been quite clear about that just a minute ago, in citing no less than Freud. Second, as far as regards the place in which each of us finds himself at present, consider my professional education and training, on the one hand, and just to cite one example, your family history, on the other: paternal grandfather with a mania for airplanes, father, suicide by jumping off a bell tower, a rather uncommon way to kill oneself; finally, mother killed by an obscure malady but certainly voluntarily. And then you, an industrialist after all, who instead of dedicating himself to the company's production, to the well-being of his workers, as your duty would require . . ."

"My duty?" Augustus the Second interrupted him vigorously.

The colloquy was gradually taking on the characteristic features of an exchange of ideas between equals, something quite positive from a therapeutic point of view, except that it was happening too soon, according to the professional principles and practice of Doctor Caroniti. A difficult patient, this Signor Valle, with whom it was perhaps opportune to be patient, in addition to being clever, naturally. So he responded to him with a beaming smile, "To tell the truth, from an ethical perspective, or even from the primary psychological one, duties in that sense don't exist. But as you certainly understand, our lives are inserted in an environment, in an order, in a system I would say if the word were not so discredited, and in any case, the principle is valid everywhere and in whatever regime, and the system, the others, expect that we will conduct ourselves coherently, to the advantage of all. From me, for example, they expect that I will treat the mentally ill, and I do treat them. From you, they expect that you will enhance productivity, that you will manufacture a larger quantity of buttons, maybe even plastic buttons, and instead you squander your time talking to birds."

"I knew I would be persecuted on account of my love for birds," Augustus the Second mumbled with a heavy heart.

"Admit that it's not normal," the psychiatrist insisted. "And let's not talk about the three million lire donated to Italia Nostra. Total madness!"

On hearing the reference to the three million lire, which probably weighed a little even on his own conscience, Augustus the Second took offense. "There are those who spend three million on a new car," he declared. "What is your opinion of people who spend three or even six million on a new car, and then they go out and kill themselves in it?"

At this point, the colloquy, which had developed into an exchange between equals, went back to being an exchange between unequals but now all to the advantage of Augustus the Second, who displayed a dangerous tendency to reversing the established roles. It was time to restore order, with kindness, yes, but also with resolve. "Signor Valle," the psychiatrist asked amiably, "Signor Valle, is it I who has to examine you, or you who has to examine me?"

Augustus the Second had the impression that the whole thing was coming apart and that this would only benefit his wife, Palmira. It behooved him to back off, even in the face of this psychiatrist, who was so full of contradictions. "Excuse me," he said humbly. "I must go along."

"Bravo, bravo," Doctor Caroniti hastened to say, by now a bit tired. "Go back to the ward now and calmly do what they tell you to do."

Augustus the Second, in truth more tired than the doctor, thanked him and got up to leave. But slowly and pensively. And in fact, before going out, he turned to ask, "I don't want to cause any disturbance, but can I have my lawyer come here to see me?"

"Lawyer," Doctor Caroniti repeated, caught by surprise. Then he regained his composure and said, "Certainly, certainly, we're not in jail here." To make an end of it, as a clever psychiatrist, he corrected himself humorously, "Then again, lawyers go to jails, too. On the contrary, that's where they belong."

Chapter the Eleventh

In which Augustus the Second,
despite many misadventures,
maintains all of his decorum.

Early on in his hospital stay, Augustus the Second was subjected to scrupulous examinations and rigorous testing.
They conducted, for example, an analysis of his urine, color
straw yellow, and clear consistency, minimal traces of albu-
min and hematic pigment, absence of mucopus, absence of
glucose, absence of acetone, absence of bile pigments, and a
lot of other things. They also performed a lipoprotein pro-
file, with alpha and beta and pre-beta lipoproteins, beta-
alpha ratio normal, serum aspect clear, and a lot of other
things. They even prescribed a blood test, with the Hanger
flocculation reaction, the Kunkel phenol reaction, and the
McLagan turbidity reaction, and the Takata reaction, as
well as the Wunderly and Wuhrmann reaction, and the

Katz index. They did bacteria cultures. They gave him an electrocardiogram and, of course, an electroencephalogram. They tapped his joints with hammers to check his reflexes. Moreover, they supplied him, morning and night, with a good quantity of pills and capsules, all very colorful. Finally, they executed an unbelievable number of enteroclysms or enemas.

Owing to his natural disingenuousness but also because he was disoriented by the novelty and exceptionality of his environment, he was inclined to believe that the enemas were—he was subjected to so many of them—a form of psychotherapy aimed at wringing out of his spirit his inordinate passion for birds, just as he was inclined to play endless card games or chess matches with some fellow inmate, or to listen with rapt attention to the accounts of a guy who had fought at the Battle of Waterloo, on the side of Napoleon, naturally. "We're there," he would say every so often, without overdoing the drama, even though he used that phrase to remark to himself his unmistakable progress toward a state of dementia, or mental alienation.

In effect, in his internal relationships with the other inmates, or with the nurses, or the doctors, he was gradually losing, by dint of his constantly going along, if not his powers of reason at least his will to fight. But he found it again, instantly and almost effortlessly, as soon as he came into contact with the outside world.

It had happened, for example, the day they called him to the reception area and, in a small adjacent room, rather dismal even for an asylum, he found the venerable attorney Alessandro Mantini, who, before becoming his lawyer, had been his poor grandfather's lawyer. In fact, it was none other than he who had helped draft his grandfather's famous will and testament and, who knows, maybe even influenced him, and imagine how fond he was of Augustus the Second, and imagine how much Augustus the Second knew he could trust him. He still called him Grandpa Mantini, as he had when he was a little boy.

The grand old man had tears in his eyes and his voice trembled from emotion as well as old age when he said to Augustus the Second that he never would have expected to find him in a place like that. "You'd be better off in jail," he said. He was a man of acute intelligence, still healthy constitution, and an optimistic outlook.

"Grandpa Mantini," Augustus the Second said to him, "is it possible that a man can be thrown into a loony bin like this without knowing why and without having done anything strange?"

"It's possible," the old man declared. "Don't think for a minute that I haven't studied your case very carefully. The law is on the side of your wife."

"That's one hell of a damned law," Augustus the Second couldn't stop himself from saying.

"*Summum jus, summa injuria*, as Cicero was wont to say, supreme law is supreme injury."

Augustus the Second pondered that for a minute. Then he said, "You're right, Grandpa Mantini. It would have been better to end up in jail. If they throw you in jail, at least, sooner or later, they have to give you a trial. Here, no way. They can keep you prisoner until judgment day without anyone being able even to stick their nose in."

"That's pretty much the way it is. The doctors will have to file a report with the court, but they have a month to do it, and really, no one is going to second-guess their evaluation. You're in their hands, son."

Once again, Augustus the Second took a moment to ponder, and then he proposed, "We could go assemble the evidence that Doctor Colbiati has been my wife's lover for two years."

The venerable lawyer shook his head. "You know, the doctor probably had a lot of good reasons to want to do your wife a favor; I'm not saying he didn't. Objectively speaking, however, he had a dozen good reasons to do it for her. Let's start with your ancestors. Your grandfather, bless his soul, nobody knew him better than I did. He was good and in his own way, ingenious, but good heavens was he strange; you can't imagine how strange. And let's not even talk about your father. His only act of volition in his entire life was throwing himself off a bell tower and mortgaging your future with his suicide. Your mother, mean beyond belief."

"But so what if they were crazy? Does that mean I belong in a lunatic asylum?"

"The sins of the fathers are often visited upon their children, and this is one of those times. But look at you, too, for your part . . . the three million donated to Italia Nostra . . . the fake mustache. . . . What got into your head, managing a business with a fake mustache!"

"That way, it was easy for them to see that I was exactly like my grandfather, and so they wouldn't keep breaking my balls with innovations."

"But meanwhile, you ended up in the lunatic asylum."

"But meanwhile, they haven't been able to make any innovations. I am still the boss, aren't I?"

"You are, but I'm not sure for how much longer. It's clear that your wife wants to have you declared incompetent. But it's equally clear that we will oppose it. We'll go all the way to the supreme court, if need be. It'll take them years to beat us, if indeed they do beat us."

As the old man was saying this, Augustus the Second envisioned him as at least touched by immortality, but he was too preoccupied with his own problems to feel happy about it. "Grandpa Mantini," he asked sadly, "in the meantime, will I have to stay locked up in the asylum?"

"You, my dear, have to be patient. And prudent, too. Keep your eyes wide open. You can bet they'll be going on the attack, and soon, I'd say. Listen to me. Don't sign anything, not even a postcard, if I don't authorize you to. Promise me that."

"I promise. But in the meantime, couldn't you do something to get me out of here?"

"We'll leave no stone unturned," the old man proclaimed solemnly. Then a thought went through his mind, a happy thought, judging from the expression on his face. "But you"— he came over to say almost in Augustus the Second's ear— "did you really do all those filthy things with your wife?"

Augustus the Second turned red from shame. "She even pulled out our bedroom secrets?"

"Everything. Everything that might damage you. Now, it's not that I'm easily scandalized. Everyone, just about . . . although I, by now . . . But in your case, you know, one thing on top of another. . . . Now it's up to you to show, as far as you can, that you're normal. I implore you: your sexual behavior must be unexceptionable."

"Here there's no danger. The place is full of monsters."

"No fake mustache . . ."

"I left it at home."

Finally, for his third recommendation, the aging lawyer pulled out the rule about the birds: "And above all, no birds," he said. "For the love of God, don't start cavorting with the birds here, too, otherwise there's no way you'll ever get out of here."

"Okay," Augustus the Second mumbled sadly. The colloquy was over; all that was left to do was give the old man a hug and take his leave. But as he hugged him, he asked him one last question: "Tell me the truth, Grandpa Mantini. Do I seem really crazy?"

"Well, a little crazy, yes." The old man smiled. "But who isn't?"

So Augustus the Second went back to join the crazy people thinking that the old man was really right: everyone in this world was a little crazy but some, a few, were shut inside and the rest were outside, and he was among the few who were inside, and he was going to be there a long time, as far as he could tell, maybe even all the way to the end of his earthly life, as his wife, Palmira, had taken the opportunity to announce to him.

Their colloquy had taken place not in the dreary little room near the reception but in the office of Doctor Caroniti himself, where, aside from his desk, the chairs, the books, and the pictures, there was also a couch. All Augustus the Second had to do was go in, take a look at his wife and a look at the couch, and he was able to deduce, rightly, that Doctor Caroniti had just fucked her. The thing didn't upset him in the least with respect to his affections, given that he hadn't desired his wife for a long time now, but from a, so to speak, diagnostic point of view, it was certainly not an advantage.

Signora Palmira had dressed to the nines for that visit, a sunflower print silk dress, which enhanced her glorious curves. She was even in a good mood. "Doctor Caroniti," she said spritely, "is just so nice, plus he really likes you."

"I imagine he likes you a lot, too," Augustus the Second observed gallantly.

And she, having grasped the mild irony, replied without taking offense, "Why, is there some reason he shouldn't? All things considered, I'm not exactly a throwaway."

"I'd throw you away," Augustus the Second said to her jokingly. "But I can't. The law is on your side."

Signora Palmira had made, recently too, considerable progress in her climb to bourgeois status. So instead of throwing a shoe at her husband as she would have in her better days, she smiled gracefully and changed the subject. "Doctor Caroniti tells me that you are behaving very well. If you keep it up, you'll be out of here soon. Soon, in a manner of speaking, however. It takes time, you know, for all the tests, the treatment."

"I know," Augustus the Second admitted ironically.

"Back at the factory, we're doing our best to keep things on course," she said. "We really had no idea just how precious your work was. It seemed like you weren't doing anything, but instead it was all you."

"Well, I don't know about that," Augustus the Second allowed with the utmost modesty.

"You may not know it, but we do," Signora Palmira declared with appropriate zest. "You don't have any idea how many times a day we get into trouble. Not because we don't know what to do, but because we can't do it without your consent. So, for the good of us all, I brought you this paper to sign. It's nothing, just a simple power of attorney. After all, I am your wife, aren't I?"

She held out the document to Augustus the Second, but he didn't want to take it. "I'm not signing anything," he said matter-of-factly.

"What does that mean?"

"You understood perfectly. I'm not signing anything unless my lawyer tells me to."

"Your lawyer? Since when do you have a lawyer?"

"Since I was born," Augustus the Second replied unabashedly. "His name is Alessandro Mantini, his office is in Milan, and you can't fuck him. He's over ninety."

Signora Palmira couldn't believe it. She couldn't believe, that is, the aggressive resistance of that jerk of a husband of hers. Had he really gone crazy? If so, then it was only right that he was where he was. "Remember this," she said conclusively. "Remember this well because you're hearing it from Palmira Radice: the only way you'll ever get out of here is feet first."

"I don't give a fuck," Augustus the Second replied decorously. "I like it here."

Chapter the Twelfth

In which, for Augustus the Second,
a little light shines down from heaven.

Now that he had so solemnly committed himself, Augustus the Second had to like it in the asylum willy-nilly. Actually, he wasn't so bad off there when he managed to adapt. But sometimes, toward evening—that is, about the time it made him feel bad to hear a church bell crying over the end of the day—his heart was made even more tender by thoughts of little Giuseppe, or of the birds in the gardens, or, as is more likely, of little Giuseppe providing for the birds in the gardens. A wet and rainy November descended on his spirit and he was invaded by a pungent melancholy, but it had to be taken into account that in an asylum, melancholy is, without a doubt, the least of misfortunes so that, all in all, comparing himself to the others, he might even find some reason for consolation.

Consolation that was, however, ephemeral, since if, as was evident, the others were sick and he wasn't, what legitimate reason could they possibly have for keeping him in there? As far as he was able to understand, apart from the colorful little pills morning and night, apart from the enemas they continued to lavish on him the minute his bowels failed to move on their own, and we might as well add, apart from the every-other-day colloquies with Doctor Caroniti, there was nothing going on in that lunatic asylum that was important for him unless one was to consider important and beneficial to his mental health his exchanges of opinion with the paranoid who wanted to swim to the United States, or his pointless card games and chess matches.

There was, therefore, a sort of complicated injustice that was being committed to his detriment. He was well aware of that, but he also knew that in order to have even a tenuous probability of getting out of that trap alive, he had to go along with, or in plain words, perilously cooperate with, those who had trapped him.

Now, there not being for the moment any other prospect and not wanting to end up in the agitated ward, he was open to anything. Yet it was not always easy, or simple, to go along, especially when it involved Doctor Caroniti, who, in truth, was always involved. Indeed, it seemed that Doctor Caroniti, by fate or by the concurrence of foreordained circumstances, was destined to become a sort of overlord of his body and soul, both severally and jointly, and that he was aiming to achieve that with every means at his disposal, from the colorful pills to the laborious and by all appearances off-the-wall colloquies they had every other day, which, scientifically, went by the name of psychotherapy.

For this psychotherapy to reach any positive outcome whatsoever, it was indispensable that in the course of the sessions, Augustus the Second should talk by way of free association—that is, by attaching one idea to another, or one image to another, or even an image to an idea or an idea to an image, catch as catch can, without so much as thinking about it. To Augustus the Second, it seemed too good to be true that he could be cured by talking at random, jumping from one subject to another as he had always been inclined to do. Except that it invariably happened that his free associations ended up going to the birds, and Doctor Caroniti would get upset. To tell the truth, if he had been a good psychotherapist, there would have been no need for him to get upset, but he had fucked his patient's wife, and by now, his being a good psychotherapist, in this specific case, was no longer in the cards.

He gave it everything he had, poor guy, but with negligible results. For example, he would set down a blank sheet of paper in front of Augustus the Second, give him a pencil, and ask him to draw lickety-split the first thing that came into his head. Augustus the Second avoided the temptation to draw one of his passerines, and he would make a nice drawing of a house, or a tree, or the sea, but then voom, he would put some birds in. And Doctor Caroniti would get upset because, according to him, the birds were a sign of illness.

"But," Augustus the Second rebutted quite reasonably, "is it possible to imagine a house or a tree without passerines or the sea without seagulls?"

Deep down inside, Doctor Caroniti had to agree that it wasn't possible, but it bothered him, and so he moved on, with even less probability of good results, to the second phase of the treatment—that is, the re-education of the patient.

According to him, Augustus the Second, surely as a reaction to the shipwreck that his parents had been, longed for the absolute, for perfection, and it seemed that nothing was as paralyzing as perfectionism, which could even become a convenient alibi for impotence. There it was, by his stubborn insistence on keeping the button factory up to the standard—as he saw it of the perfection reached by his grandfather—Augustus the Second had become fossilized. The world had not stood still in the era of his proto-aviator grandfather, and so why did Augustus the Second have to be stuck there? He needed to progress. But if he was to progress, he had to abandon his paralyzing perfectionism and accept compromise with vivifying reality. Compromise, the psychiatrist declared, was the ideal meeting point between the individual and his environment, consisting not in approaching things as a bull, with your head down and crashing through them with your horns, but in taking things in the right way, going around them if necessary, and moving beyond.

Augustus the Second didn't like that comparison to horns at all and not because he felt diminished in his own spiritual value by the circumstance that his wife allowed herself to be fucked even by psychiatrists but because it was evident that Doctor Caroniti intended to corrupt his integrity and, deep down, to undermine his resistance in order to achieve the objective of having him hand over the factory to his wife. Augustus the Second understood very well that the doctor had some such aim, not wholly on the up-and-up from the medical point of view, because in fact the doctor had his wife but didn't have the factory, while he, who had the factory but not his wife, was naturally inclined to keep the factory and even more so the gardens behind it, where his birds were still living.

It was all too clear that in these circumstances, Doctor Caroniti was in for some major professional difficulties, and he actually suffered from drastic mood changes, created a lot of confusion, and navigated amid tremendous uncertainties, and thank goodness Augustus the Second was in his hands, not because he was really ill but because he had been pushed there by a malicious wife, otherwise who knows how things would have gone.

In effect, a good psychotherapist, or caretaker of souls, must, while maintaining an opportune position of authority vis-à-vis his patient, compromise himself with him and compromise himself by loving him, by taking upon himself, so to speak, his patient's anxieties, and Doctor Caroniti was unable to do this because of the well-known incident with Signora Palmira, to a degree that quite often, of the two, he was the one more full of anxieties but his own particular anxieties, because he suffered from a feeling of guilt that dragged him insanely into humiliating himself before Augustus the Second, until one day he reached the point, he of all people, of singing the praises of the birds to him.

He began by reciting for him a long piece of a poem by the supreme poet Giacomo Leopardi, which spoke of a solitary sparrow that sang, with surprising expertise, of the manic-depressive syndrome. Then he said that taking loving care of birds was the sign of an elevated and sensitive spirit, perhaps even too much so, and that in any case, there were no people in the world so contemptible as those who, armed with a shotgun, went around killing harmless little birds. In sum, the good psychiatrist had also set out on the road of free association, on his way, perhaps, even to considering the three million donated to Italia Nostra in a good light, but he realized it in time and did an about-face, concluding unexpectedly that when one has a family and a button factory to run, he must dedicate himself first and foremost to the buttons and then, if he has extra time, to the birds.

In different circumstances, Augustus the Second would have remained silent, but Doctor Caroniti's foregoing little speech had gotten him a little too worked up, and so he said, in total confidence, that to him, birds were a lot more than passion and distraction and that he had relied on them many times to help him manage the factory.

On hearing this, Doctor Caroniti immediately regained his composure—that is, he assumed again the air of someone who frequents, for professional purposes, the insane. "How's that again?" he hastened to ask.

"You see," Augustus the Second patiently explained, "birds, for the fact that they fly up there in the sky, are closer than we are to the gods, and so, in certain circumstances, they can serve as intermediaries between the gods and us, make the celestial will known to earthlings. Oftentimes, in antiquity, before fighting a war or founding a city, men took it upon themselves to find out what the gods thought about it, and the gods, for their part, let them know what they thought about it by means of the birds. In the same way, I, through the birds, was able to get advice about what I should do with the factory. You have to admit, compared to fighting a war or founding a city like Rome, running a button factory is child's play."

"You mean to say," Doctor Caroniti started to ask with astonishment unworthy of a psychiatrist, "you mean to say that you organized the production of your factory according to suggestions you were given by the birds?"

Augustus the Second would have been glad to make him believe that, but then he thought that it might not be wise. To tell the truth, it wasn't easy deciding what was the best thing to do in that ugly misadventure of the lunatic asylum: to make them think he was crazy or to make them think he was sane. Making them think he was crazy meant, at the very least, being declared incompetent, with the consequence that he would lose control of the factory and its gardens, but once they had achieved that, they would surely let him out.

Making them think he was sane, on the other hand, meant staying in there for the rest of his life, in accordance with the wishes of Signora Palmira. In his uncertainty, Augustus the Second muddled through as best he could, going first one way and then the other, trying not to go too far out on a limb either way.

But he didn't always manage to do that, poor guy. Like the day that, as Doctor Caroniti was holding forth for the umpteenth time on the magnificent advantages of compromise, he saw outside the window behind the doctor a finch sitting on the branch of a beech tree. "Hey, Leopoldo's here!" he exclaimed.

"Who's here?" Doctor Caroniti asked apprehensively.

By now, it was too late to turn back. "Leopoldo," he repeated. "There he is, right there."

Doctor Caroniti turned and saw the finch, or maybe he didn't even see it. To him, the appalling thing was not that there should be a bird sitting on a branch but something else, and he was asking Augustus the Second for an explanation with a look that was steadily turning sterner.

"I told him not to come," muttered Augustus the Second all confused. "I told him he would get me into a lot of trouble." Then he recovered his dignity and said, "If he came, there must be some reason. Maybe he has something to tell me."

He stood up and turned toward the bird, assuming the posture of Saint Francis in the famous fresco, and modulated a long melodious whistle, composed of several notes.

From outside, the finch sang him an intense little cantata and flew away.

Then Augustus the Second turned to look at his psychiatrist and said to him, "Now I know something wonderful is about to happen to me."

Chapter the Thirteenth

In which, for Augustus the Second,
the heavenly light shines brighter.

After the episode of the exchange of views with the finch which, truthfully, seen in a realistic light, was rather disturbing, Doctor Caroniti began to doubt whether the stay in the asylum and the treatment so generously administered so far would ever lead to any progress for his patient, Augustus the Second. Not that he was thinking of releasing him, not that, not even remotely, quite the contrary; after that freakish whistling, it was more than ever the case to keep him locked up. But it was time to conjure up a new approach.

Augustus the Second was an unusual patient; as soon as he was pigeonholed, not without considerable effort, into some diagnostic compartment, there he was, suddenly popping up in what appeared to be the opposite compartment.

All things considered, his was an obscure and even totally new case, seeing as nobody had ever thought of submitting Saint Francis to a psychiatric examination, as would perhaps have been opportune. A case, nevertheless, that stimulated the scientific and imaginative disposition of Doctor Caroniti. He puzzled over it for several days, arrived at the discovery that idleness is the root of all evil, and therefore also of mental illness, and concluded that it was fitting that he rescue Augustus the Second from idleness.

He proposed to Augustus that he take charge of the mail.

Handling the mail was not a big job, naturally, since there are very few sane people who write to crazy people and even fewer crazy people who write to other crazy people, but from fifteen to twenty missives, between letters and postcards, including those that some of the inmates wrote to themselves, arrived each day, and Augustus the Second managed to spend an entire morning sorting them and subdividing them and even possibly reading them, after which he saw to their distribution.

This brought him into contact not only with his fellow male inmates but also with the female inmates in the ward reserved for them. Unfortunately, it appeared that between feminine grace and beauty, on the one hand, and mental illness, on the other, there existed some arcane opposition. The madwomen, in other words, were all ugly. Nevertheless, taking them in the right way, they were, besides being different from the men, also more amusing, especially the ones who liked to look at, and maybe even touch, the men's private parts. He learned how to deal with them in a playful way. "Antonietta," he would say to one of them, "you should see what a weapon Tommaso has!"

"Tommaso was born rude," she replied. "He won't show it to me."

"Insist, insist," he exhorted her and went on his way.

Tommaso was a nurse on the women's ward, and he got very peeved over the publicity that Augustus the Second was giving him. "Be careful," he would say to him, "be careful, or one of these days I'm going to turn you over to these madwomen and then you'll see what you're in for!"

Augustus the Second wouldn't have wanted that to happen, and not only because of the ugliness and, for the most part, advanced age of those crazy women, but because ever since his wife, Palmira, had denied herself to him, his sexuality, once so uncontrollable, had totally shut down. He had gone back to the times of his infantile innocence, when he loved, intensely and almost exclusively, Our Lady of Sorrows, and went to sleep with his hands on top of the covers, as an old servant woman had taught him, *ne nos inducas in tentationem.*

Then, one day, it happened that he had to deliver a postcard addressed to a certain Signorina Serafina Bozzoli. Nothing important, naturally. It came from India, but there was nothing written on it but a few illegible signatures. He could just as well have thrown it away and nobody would have been the worse for it. He was very scrupulous, however, in performing the service that he had agreed to provide, and he went looking for this Serafina.

"Are you Serafina Bozzoli?" he asked one inmate, and she rudely answered no.

And a second and a third inmate, both of whom rudely answered no. He deduced that this Serafina must be disliked by just about everybody.

Finally, one of them responded, "Phooey on her, that whore!"

"Okay," he replied in a conciliatory tone. "But where is she?"

"She's out there, the whore," the inmate answered.

Out there was a hallway. And in the hallway, in a corner down at the far end, sitting cross-legged on the floor, with an Indian kufi on her head, all sequins and mirrors, and a tunic, also Indian, bell-bottom jeans with fringed cuffs, bare feet, her head bowed in meditation, was a young woman. "Are you Serafina Bozzoli?"

"Bozzóli," she corrected his pronunciation meekly and looked up at him.

Fair skin, framed by blond hair with bangs, that face was the sweetest face one could imagine, and her eyes were the purest eyes one could imagine, windows to the sky, and Augustus the Second had no trouble comparing her to an angel, not least because in his view, undoubtedly because of their wings, angels were the closest things in the world to birds.

But he felt like he was about to die from the shock of this bizarre turn of events. "Mail!" he managed to say in the most impersonal way and slipped the postcard between her hands.

But to her, it seemed, the postcard couldn't have mattered less. She kept her eyes riveted on him and levitated, blossoming with hope. "I was expecting you," she said softly.

Then, as if that weren't enough, she did something else that was equally extraordinary. She pulled out a flute, held it up to her mouth, blew into it, and out came a stream of birdsongs, thrush and titlark, titmouse and wheatear and short-toed treecreeper, the dulcet blackcap and the sublime nightingale, until, as the culmination, she riffed into finch, or the intense cantata of Leopoldo, and so there was no longer the shadow of a doubt that the wonderful thing that had been announced to him was now taking place. He was already in love. My God, already hopelessly in love, and since it was the first time in his life that this had happened to him, he was so overwhelmed by it that he ran away.

But Serafina smiled serenely, with her pink lips and perfectly arranged white teeth, because she knew he would come back.

Chapter the Fourteenth

*In which, despite everything,
Serafina emanates
light.*

Augustus the Second, in fact, returned to her the next day because he had to deliver another postcard. She was still sitting in the corner of the hallway and it seemed she was still in meditation, her legs crossed yoga-style and her head bowed. After spending the whole night fighting off the nightmare that he had only imagined her or that she was only the ghost of something created and not properly a created thing in flesh and blood, he couldn't, even now, feel sure that she really existed. Seeing her so motionless and fixated in a way that wasn't easy to figure out, he was almost expecting her to suddenly disappear, like the angels in the Bible story.

But she didn't disappear, and after a little while, still without lifting her eyes, with that voice of hers that resonated with paradise, she said, "I'm receiving messages."

That was fine with him; he was happy to stand there looking at her, even though, as far as he could understand, nothing was happening. Time standing still and always like this, with her sitting right before his eyes, would be all he would ever need, he was sure of it.

Then she lifted her face and smiled, and naturally, she was even more beautiful; she opened up the heavens for both of them. She took the postcard that he had been holding out to her all this time, but she didn't ignore it like she had the one from the day before. This time, she looked at it, read it, and reread it with great attention, and little by little, her heavenly smile turned into an earthly grin of enjoyment. "But you wrote this one!"

"How do you know?"

"I receive messages," she said a bit mysteriously. "Plus, there's no stamp, and only crazy people send postcards without stamps. And then it says 'I love you,' and you love me."

All of a sudden, Augustus the Second felt full of courageous exuberance. "Oh, how I love you!" he exclaimed. "Since yesterday I can't tell if I'm asleep or awake; all I do is dream of you. With eyes closed and eyes open, I dream of you constantly. But I never manage to dream you as beautiful as you really are."

She, too, was happy about this love, but for the moment, she had a sort of modesty about her own happiness. "You've got a funny name," she said, looking at the postcard again. "It sounds like the name of an emperor."

"I'm just a poor devil," he answered, "and that's never bothered me, but now it seems to me that everything is changing."

"You're not a poor devil," she said. "I can read in your eyes the ups and downs of the spiral of becoming and serenity in the sphere of harmony. You are part of my relationship with the universal, you are the image of an autonomous reality that leads me to identify myself with the symbols of my research."

Augustus the Second was listening more to her voice, which was so lovely, than to her words, which were a little obscure, but that posed no obstacle to his growing love, no obstacle at all.

"I need to purify myself," she said. "That's why I was expecting you."

To him, it seemed too beautiful to be true, and he asked, "Are you serious?"

"Naturally," she smiled, "certainly I wasn't totally sure that you would arrive yesterday, and there was no way I could predict that I would find you in a lunatic asylum, or that you would have your same mouth and eyes. But as soon as I saw you, I knew it was you."

"Me?" said Augustus the Second, somewhat dismayed. His dismay, naturally, did not come from the banal suspicion that she had mistaken him for another or from an inkling that she was, after all, really a bit mad but rather from the fear that he was not at all what she was thinking; *non dignus, Domine.* "I don't think I can help anything or anyone."

"You have the signs of the spirit," she said with simple conviction. "Your soul is much closer than mine to the great cosmic spirit."

"Closer than yours is impossible. You're an angel."

She shook her head, still marvelously angelic, even though she wished to deny it. "I've made too many mistakes in my life," she said. "I've never meditated enough. Rarely have

I risen from the instinctive level to the spiritual level. I have denied myself to the calls of the great spirit. I haven't listened to the messages that have come to me from the universe, or by way of the universe. I've even treated my body badly. Look." She lifted up her Indian blouse, and she had a big scar on her belly that went all the way around to her left side. "I don't know if I really wanted to die," she said. "I jumped from the fourth floor. My body was left profaned. Our body comes to us from God; it must not be profaned."

"Are you crippled?" he asked.

"What a strange idea." She laughed. "But I was fifteen when I did this, and my body was not yet fully formed. I would have grown taller, more beautiful. Now I'm sorry."

"To me, you're even too beautiful," he said. "You must be beautiful inside, too. You have the countenance of an angel. And your name is Serafina. Do you ever think about that?"

She thought about it, but she was amused by her name. It was funny, albeit not as funny as Augustus the Second. "My face is like this because it reflects my desire for purification," she said. "But the rest of my body recalls my faults. And besides, I haven't always made love with love. A lot of times I've done it with anger, with a desire to abandon myself to fate, or with distraction, which is even worse. If I died now, I could reincarnate as a soldier, a merchant, or a servant of power, and it would be a regression. But I want to progress, assure the continuation of universal values, advance toward pure existence. Now God has sent you to me. You will help me; that's what you have come to do."

"You scare me."

"What are you scared of?"

"Of not being up to it. What am I supposed to do?"

"Nothing. Be who you are."

"I've always been who I am, and it's never gone well for me. Look where I've ended up, in a lunatic asylum."

"Here or anywhere else, to the spirit it's all the same."

"I know. But before you came, this place was very ugly."

Now, however, it had become the most beautiful place in the world because there was a new happiness to be known there, never dreamed of before. With his son, they hadn't allowed him enough time to be happy. And as for the birds, he certainly couldn't complain, but the happiness one can feel with birds is like the happiness one feels with poetry or with prayer; an intense happiness there's no doubt about that, but all in all, a little precarious, and in the end, you realize that a large portion of human substance is left out of it unutilized.

But Serafina got all of him involved, every part of him in his entirety and all the parts together, even though, angel that she was, one certainly couldn't think of doing something, carnally speaking. But touching her with your fingertips was allowed, light caresses of her hands or her cheeks, even of her lips, just to feel if she was real; and consolation was born of it. Sometimes, it seemed, hope was born of it, too, although it was hard to know for what, given that what they possessed already had an absolute fullness to it, and a greater sense of well-being couldn't be imagined. Not by him, surely.

Now, during recreation hour, she came outside, too. They sat down together on a bench, and they stayed there for the whole time holding hands. Sometimes a passerine came by to say festively how happy the whole genus was about what was happening to them, and they didn't send him away. On the contrary, they exchanged a few phrases with a whistle or with the flute that she always brought along with her. By now, getting out of there or not was of very little interest to them. The nurses, given their motionless chastity, didn't bother them, and even the inmates left them in peace because true love is a sentiment respected by all living beings and by crazy people even more than others. "I'm trying to remember where I first met you," she said.

Despite being head over heels, he was still rather anchored to phenomenal reality. "I've never moved from the place where I was born," he said. "Just once, when I went to Assisi."

She shook her head but with the usual sweetness, without reproach for his limited sensibility. "As soon as I saw you, I recognized you. I knew you were you," she said. "I must have met you in an earlier life."

He had never considered the question of earlier lives, and if, as was possible, he had touched shoulders with sainthood, he had taken it lightly, without really focusing or digging too deep. But now that he came to think of it, there might just be something out there or up above. After all, didn't she communicate with Leopoldo, too, and with who knows how many other birds? And wasn't she a total marvel? Didn't she have the face of an angel?

Now he, too, started trying to conjure up his earlier lives. One day, he confided to her that in all likelihood, he was a reincarnation of his grandfather Augustus, and she allowed as how that could well be the case, but when she found out that his grandfather Augustus had died after he was born, she said no because souls migrate and are reincarnated only after the death of those who carry them.

Little by little, a little one day and a little the next, they got to know each other better and love each other more. They told each other their stories but with a way of talking that was rarified, muffled, cadenced by long pauses of silence and meditation. A way of talking that taken altogether, was more birdlike than human.

"What's got into you?"

"What do you mean what's got into me?"

"What's wrong?"

"Wrong? Nothing."

"Me neither, nothing."

In the end, they couldn't remember who had posed the first question or who had answered this way or that. Anyway, it didn't make any difference because they were now one and the same, two spirits in one, or better, two bodies with just one soul.

"My father makes loads of money," she would say. "And my mother spends the loads of money that my father makes. I hate them both."

He didn't feel like he had a whole lot to tell about his own family. That his father had been very good to him perhaps, and his mother very mean, without perhaps, but he had never really loved the one or really hated the other. Not even after she had lied to him about the paternity of his son, Giuseppe, had he got to the point of hating his mother; anyway, it certainly wasn't worth it to hate a dead woman. But Serafina's parents were still living; probably they were as mean as his wife, Palmira, was, so it was actually right to hate them.

"But when I was little," she said, "I was so in love with my father. At night, the times that he could take me into his bed, I sprinkled myself all over with talcum powder to smell good and put on my best nightgown. I thought I would marry him when I grew up. Later, the hate set in. He's a pig; all he thinks about is making money."

Then she said, "This is the third time I've ended up in the loony bin. The first time was when I fell from the third floor, but that wasn't an asylum like this one; it was a luxury clinic in Switzerland. The second time was a luxury clinic, too. My father had me locked up because I was causing him problems with his workers. At the clinic, I gave myself to everyone, anybody who wanted me. It was a bad use of my body, I know, but I didn't like myself at all back then. I could have died even. Then one of the doctors fell in love with me and we ran off. I was still a minor. When they caught up with us, he went to jail because my father refused to forgive him. And I ended up here. It's harder to escape from here. Plus, I don't really want to; I'm in a period of concentration."

Then she said, "I went to jail once, too. In London. I went shoplifting at Marks & Spencer. But the judge let me out right away; he liked me. They didn't even make me leave the country."

Then she went on, "I have a brother. I loved him so much, with my whole self. We actually made love, you know. For almost a year. Now, I don't remember it at all. He went to work for my father. Now all he thinks about is making money, too."

Then she said, "In Paris, two years ago, I was living with Dominique and César. I loved Dominique. I still love him. In fact, he sends me messages sometimes. I loved César, too, naturally, but I really hurt him bad. César was Black; he was from Ethiopia. We were going to have a kid, but then I got an abortion."

Then she said, "I had abortions two other times, and it didn't bother me at all. But I loved César, and having a kid with him would have been good. Now when I see little kids, I start crying sometimes."

While she was telling him these things, Augustus never took his eyes off her, off her mouth. If he had let her talk without looking at her, in all likelihood he would have been overwhelmed by the enormity of the enterprise of trying to lift up a soul so weighed down by bad experiences. But looking at her, seeing her face, despite everything, emanating the light of her angelic essence, no one could lose heart. On the contrary, you got to the point of perceiving a certain positivity in sin, so evident that, in the end, just as death was the necessary precondition of any resurrection, so sin was a sort of indispensable platform for anyone who wished to ascend to the ultimate redemption or spiritualization, as she preferred to call it. So all in all, in the task he had taken on, for better or worse, of participating in her purification, he ended up feeling inadequate, or in other words, he had come to think of himself as being not quite sinful enough. So to make up for that, he tried to highlight the few instances of profane and materialistic behavior that he had to offer. "With my wife," he confessed to her one day, "I, I made love in the filthiest way."

"When you love someone," she responded serenely, "there are no filthy ways of making love."

"But I didn't love her. She turned me on sensually, and that's it."

"Then it was not elevated love."

"You see how base I am. I need purification, too."

"We have met so we can help each other," she said, and by now, there was not a reason in the world to doubt it.

Chapter the Fifteenth

In which a pair of angels,
after a long flight through the purest of skies,
glide onto a pile of hay.

According to Serafina—who by some unknown route had come into contact with Tibetan mysticism—words were mantras, that is, instruments for thinking, and naturally also for knowing and communicating, but it was not good to overuse them, especially during a time of concentration, so as not to belittle them. Primary words were concepts and mystical sounds, while belittled words served for narration and other minor tasks. And when someone, being absorbed in concentration, was totally given over to the word as concept, they would only very reluctantly stoop to the level of the narrative word. The things Serafina said, therefore, she said them a little at a time, and there were days in which she remained utterly silent.

Augustus the Second had learned to wait without impatience. He, too, was beginning to give time that all-in-all insignificant value that can only be given by those who, thanks to reincarnations, have as much of it lying before them as they want. From her, he lovingly accepted everything, from silence to confession, without letting anything surprise him anymore.

Only once did he get somewhat disoriented, when she told him that she owned a large estate near Pavia, on the banks of the River Ticino. The estate was called La Finca, and it was really all hers because she had inherited it from her maternal grandmother. But her father had never signed it over to her. He kept it for himself to go hunting.

Augustus the Second was brusquely taken aback. "Hunting?" he replied, perhaps hoping he had not heard correctly.

"Yes. They raise pheasants and partridges there, and when the hunting season opens, they shoot them."

Augustus the Second felt a rush of fear of cold and rainy November, terror at having to return to those gloomy melancholy feelings that by now he was sure he was no longer able to bear. Not even if Serafina were found to be involved in it would he be able to overlook fowling or any other supposedly aristocratic form of hunting. "Do you go hunting?" he asked, his voice quivering.

"One time, I went along."

"And did you kill?" he asked, almost in a panic.

She shook her head, marvelously as usual. "No, I cried," she said. "Out of pity and pain and for our abject state. It was then, a few days later, that I jumped out the third-story window."

Augustus the Second realized that this was it; he had overcome the last imaginable obstacle. He would love her for all eternity, even in their eventual reincarnations.

Serafina's father, that ruthless killer of pheasants and partridges, was a famous publisher. He printed lots of books and periodicals, and he knew how to sell what he printed, so he made a pile of money. He had a huge printing plant, enormous machines, employed a large number of workers. When she was little, Serafina had the impression that her father had a fantastic job. Sure, she knew he was an industrialist, but instead of making pipes or fertilizer, he made books, and it was as though he was working to make the world more beautiful and more just.

Serafina had held on to these ideas for a pretty long time, and maybe, inept as she was at understanding the way the world works, she would have held on to them even longer if she had not been caught up in a little incident that had, so to speak, forced her to come to her senses. She was a freshman in high school at the time and very pretty, and not surprisingly, whenever she happened to walk by, everyone's heads turned to look at her, and there wasn't a rich kid in all of Milan who wouldn't have been happy, given her family's wealth, to marry her or even just to go to bed with her.

She, instead, was in love with Maurizio. Maurizio didn't have a dime, and he didn't even have a surname that could take the place of money. But he did have long hair, and an Indian earring sticking out of his left earlobe, and a firm conviction that life was not worth living. He was practically always on the brink of suicide, and in the meantime, he smoked marijuana and wrote a lot of very sad poems.

In Serafina's judgment, Maurizio's poems were not only very sad but also very beautiful. She encouraged him to write more of them, and when, in not that much time really, he had enough of them in hand to make up a volume, she took them to her father so he could make a book out of them. Before turning them into a book, however, the publisher Bozzoli first had the poems examined by his experts, both artistic and financial, and then he told his daughter that he was an industrialist and not a patron of the arts for struggling imbeciles.

Serafina didn't bother to reply. She went looking for Maurizio, who lived in a rent-free attic in the Brera section of Milan, and there she smoked marijuana and let him make love to her.

It was the first time that Serafina had smoked marijuana and also the first time she had been fucked. Before that, they had only touched her and petted her, ever since she was little, friends, cousins, brothers, and servants, and it didn't bother her at all that they petted her; she liked it. But with Maurizio, she went all the way for the first time, and she got syphilis.

Augustus the Second, who was not accustomed to such diseases, gave a start and said, "Syphilis?"

"Syphilis is nothing," she declared. "A few days of antibiotics and it's over."

That was possible. Indeed, if Serafina said so, then it was certainly the case. But she had been unlucky, and he told her so. "You were unlucky."

She agreed but not so much for the syphilis but rather for the rancor she still felt toward her father who had refused to publish those beautiful poems. And Maurizio, naturally, seeing as her father was a dirty capitalist pig, had left. He'd gone off to Amsterdam, or to some other place not as culturally deprived as Milan, and took with him his poetic vein, his syphilis, and his scant zest for living.

She had been left alone to hate her father. Now she saw him in the right perspective. If he had been in the pipe or fertilizer business, that would have been fine. But like this, he was a traitor; he was pretending to be something he wasn't. And she went into rebellion. She went to march in all the leftist demonstrations, threw rocks and spit insults at the police, and got herself arrested so that her name would be printed in the newspapers. The daughter of the famous publisher. And she used to refer to herself as the daughter of the dirty capitalist. Poetry was a commodity, culture was a commodity, a writer something to be sold. If he couldn't be sold, he wasn't a writer. Risks were not to be taken. If push came to shove, bribes were paid. Intellectual power, political power, even religious power, everything could be bought and corrupted by the mighty publisher Bozzóli.

But he couldn't manage to corrupt his daughter. She was a whore, his daughter. Every evening when the waves of workers came streaming out of the plant, she would appear in front of the gates with an enormous placard: "Why do you let yourselves be exploited? The owner is a pig!" She lived under his roof, ate his bread, made him spend tons of money on her, and then she did this. He called the police. They came and picked her up, but then they released her. What she was doing was protected by the constitution, they said. And then he'd find her at the dinner table that same evening, wearing a three-hundred-thousand-lire dress.

In the end, she had bought herself a big Honda with the five hundred engine. She had high boots, leather pants and jacket, a helmet down to her neck, something you couldn't tell if it was male or female. But the workers at the plant knew it was the owner's daughter. She rode around in circles like a wild woman in front of the plant gates, accelerating and braking, leaning into the curves with her head and shoulders grazing over the pavement; daring spinouts and fishtails that threatened to crash into whoever got too close. And the workers who had motorcycles of their own joined right in, as though trying to outdo each other. And she dragged them along behind her to some inn way out in the country, where she paid for them all to eat and drink and then let them all fuck her. "In the name of Karl Marx," she incited them, "come fuck the owner's daughter!"

The strike that broke out at the printing plant of the mighty publisher Bozzóli shortly thereafter was really ugly. And so it was that Serafina was locked up in a clinic for the second time.

Augustus the Second listened to all these stories with inexhaustible amazement, not to say admiration. In ways so different from his and with a rigor undoubtedly superior to his own, Serafina displayed his same aversion to economic miracles. She also displayed, however, an astounding appetite for sexual experiences, and this confirmed her already suspected affinity, if not with the angels, at least with the birds, who were accustomed to coupling whenever it suited them, without even the shadow of cunning or restriction. That's how she was, miraculously beautiful and pure, whatever she might do. And by focusing above all on her evident beauty and purity, Augustus the Second, managed to keep her out of his waking thoughts of carnal desire. This, it must be understood, at the conscious level. But the ways of the unconscious, as is well known, are infinite and uncontrollable, and they reveal themselves, as is only natural, by way of our dreams.

Augustus the Second dreamed of himself and Serafina habitually. In his dreams, they were angels, or at the very least birds, who, as they flew along, sang the praises of nature and God, and just so, flying and singing, they satisfied, it seemed, all of life's duties. But one night it happened that the angel Augustus the Second and the angel Serafina, after soaring at length through the heavens singing praises, had finally and rather brusquely glided onto a pile of hay, and there they humanly coupled.

Augustus the Second didn't have the nerve to recount that dream to Serafina, and in fact, he didn't recount it to her. But she received her mysterious messages, and anyway Augustus the Second always had written on his face whatever it was he wanted to hide. "If you want to make love to me," she said, "I'd be happy to. Loving is knowing, and I would like to know you more and more."

This was such a beautiful thought that they immediately began kissing and touching and embracing each other. They felt superhumanly happy and out of this world.

However, they were not out of this world; they were in a lunatic asylum. Male and female nurses, doctors, and even administrators rushed in and separated them.

But by now, their blood had caught fire and it would never again go out.

Chapter the Sixteenth

*In which, by way of coupling,
a woman finds her man,
and vice versa.*

Yes, love was ablaze in their veins, burned so much it hurt, yearned to extinguish itself in orgasms and downward glides, and renew itself in caresses and resurgences, but love was not the stuff of lunatic asylums; they wouldn't let them do it.

If you think about it, this was a glaring contradiction. All eminent psychiatrists, from the ones who are in all the books to the ones who were corporeally present right there, such as Doctor Caroniti, pointed to sexual repression as the principle cause of human unhappiness and illness, exalted the carnal act as the most beautiful and healthiest act in the world, but nevertheless it seemed that the mentally ill, even those who were only presumed to be such, had to be excluded from all its benefits.

They just would not let them do it.

Augustus the Second was exonerated, deprived, and remanded. Exonerated, obviously, from the postal service, deprived, clearly, of his hour of recreation, remanded, naturally, to the ward for the semi-agitated, and all things considered, he was treated with a certain regard, considering that an inmate who had tried to fuck another inmate on a garden bench in front of all the other male and female inmates, who by way of contagion could have generated a pandemic, provoking high-level investigations, could just as easily have been sent to the agitated ward. But thanks only to the goodwill of the doctors, he was simply assigned to the semi-agitated, and again thanks to the goodwill of the doctors, he was aided by massive doses of psychotropic drugs, capable of placating his exuberant sexual impulses and, by the way, of relieving some of his pain, but in this they were not all that successful because he did nothing but cry and whimper, even though deep in his heart, he was sure that his love would never die.

Serafina, on the other hand, having previously accumulated far too many infractions of the regulations and good conduct, had been sent straight to the agitated section of her ward, but she wasn't the type to let that bother her. Just as Augustus the Second's resistance was indomitable but passive, hers, while equally indomitable, was aggressive, and even constructive at times, so that she nearly always found some way to get herself out of trouble.

So it happened that one night, as the asylum was enveloped in a silence so deep that even the most irreducible inmates had finally surrendered to biochemical persuasion, Augustus the Second, he too under the soporific effect of the pills, felt himself being shaken rather violently. Truth be told, the guy who had taken on the task of waking him had already been jostling him for a while with as much delicacy as he could muster, but then, given that the lummox gave no sign of getting the message and time was growing short, he had resolved to shake him with force, the way it was supposed to be done.

It took a little time before Augustus the Second realized that the person who was so stubbornly trying to wake him up was actually a friend, namely Tommaso the nurse. Nevertheless, he would still have told him to stop breaking his balls since for a while now the nurses had been doing nothing but breaking his balls. If it weren't that nurse Tommaso, while still struggling to pull him out of what was left of his sleepiness, had a spirited look of intrigue about him. He was even holding a raised finger in front of his sealed lips to make Augustus understand not to make a ruckus. Even Augustus the Second, slow as he was by nature and dazed as he was from the psychotropic drugs, realized that something important and propitious was in the offing and therefore that he'd better refrain, for the moment, from any kind of display.

"Are you awake?" nurse Tommaso whispered.

"Yes," he replied fairly convincingly.

"Then get up and follow me, and don't make any noise, if you can, otherwise I'll lose my job."

It so happened, good people, that the seraphic Serafina had corrupted nurse Tommaso, and since she had no money to corrupt him honestly, because at the moment she entered the asylum they had taken everything down to her last lira, she had corrupted him with what she had. Serafina was a prodigious girl in every sense of the word, for whom a roll in the hay was worth less than nothing, but it might also be worth more than anything. In this particular case, the one with nurse Tommaso was worth nothing, while the one with Augustus the Second could well be worth, in view of her presentiments, more than anything. Now was her chance to know for sure.

Nurse Tommaso had found nothing better to host the encounter of the two lustful lovers than a closet where they kept bags of bedsheets back from the laundry, and it had just one small window way up high, and so very little air, but on the other hand, you could throw yourself around wherever you wanted and always land on something soft. Serafina was already waiting for him there, wearing one of her Indian shirts, which covered, but not quite, her feminine charms.

"Behave yourselves and don't wake up the whole asylum on me," nurse Tommaso urged them. "I'll come back to get you in an hour."

He left, leaving them there all atremble in a darkness so dark nothing could be seen, not even shadows or semblances, but they surely had no need of illumination to find each other because that closet was truly cramped. They wouldn't have been able to take a step without bumping into each other, but it seemed to them and it was certainly true that even in a boundless black desert they would have instantly found each other because of the desires that they were emanating in waves of vital energy which, quite probably, erupt in darkness even more easily than they do in daylight, at least for those beings who are on the shy side, as was Augustus the Second. And so, a hand quickly met a face, and then another hand met a visage, which was hers, both in the act of giving and receiving, lingering almost incredulous over hair and forehead and cheeks and mouth, then longer over mouth showing yet more yearning, bodies still a bit stiff as though uncertain to join together but heartbeats already at the breaking point and blood rushing with growing force from the growing anxiety to go further by going even faster, the cherished assent to one's own desire perceived, and there, in crescendo, pleasure becomes more sincere, there, acceleration toward an undeferrable surge and increase, and so now mouth on mouth, still restrained on lingering lips the frenzy to go faster and faster, still restrained, but then immediately breaths finally joined in a deep kiss, every sensation of life by now intertwined in the intimate as longing and desire spread over every sensitive surface but also inside muscles and arteries and veins and nerve bundles, all the way down to their tips, through which they return frenetically to the surface, and then kisses elsewhere and everywhere on bodies now defense-less now tense, and the bonding prolonged to the unbearable, still suspended above the final boundaries to cross, and in the meantime to be felt and searched for with caresses until, there, a body and another body conjoined begin the jour-ney toward their imminent unity, so there, inside to search for the remote roots of life and death, distant springs of being and nonbeing, to then emerge from the unfathomable depths of being and nonbeing toward being in order not to be, oh tenderness and violence, frustration and joy, peace and tempests, nightmare and glory, and every other possible absurdity, all thrown together in a confused fusion moving toward unforeseeable summits and still further on toward the inevitable dispersion—oh! Serafina!—but together but together with misery and magnificence and still one more limit of expectation so as to come and become ever more together—oh, Serafina!—feeling the rising up from never explored darkness of your own orgasm to fill to the brim the other orgasm, ever upward toward obfuscating limits of sanctity and sin, until there, together—oh, Serafina, perpet-ual flower of eternal delight—together we reach the unreach-able culmination so proximate to death as to generate life, and there, each has gone beyond to survive, fully conscious of his own and the other's good, of his own and the other's evil, having eaten the fruit of the tree.

So they made love with love, transfusing each other.

Of the two, the first to get her breath back was Serafina, and she used it to say, "We have to get out of this lunatic asylum at all costs. I want to live every day and every night with you because you are my man."

"And you are my woman," he answered.

They both knew that they were speaking before God. Maybe not the old God, the one who so many thousands of centuries ago had, precisely because of an experience of that kind, expelled them from paradise, but before a new God, made in their own image and likeness.

Chapter the Seventeenth

*In which the art of compromise
is shown to be, when all is said and done,
liberating.*

Poor Augustus the Second did not know that, according to the statistics, no more than 3 percent of mental patients hospitalized through an emergency procedure ratified by a commitment order as, without his even so much as suspecting it, had happened to him, were released from psychiatric hospitals with a clean bill of health. If on top of that, and this was perhaps his case, the patient entered the hospital already cured—that is, practically sane rather than insane— then the chances of being released as cured were virtually nil because the doctors, before letting him out, first had to determine the reason for which he had been admitted, and a nonexistent reason is, if you think about it, much harder to figure out than an existing one.

So Augustus the Second, when he went to Doctor Caroniti to tell him that he felt really well after all the good therapies they had lavished on him and that he was even ready to return to the outside world, did not encounter the favor that in his heart he was expecting.

Doctor Caroniti looked at him with curiosity and, all things considered, benevolence. Indeed, he was delighted that for the first time this patient of his was expressing with such visible self-awareness the desire to reintegrate himself, hopefully in some productive fashion, into society, but he said, this was nothing more than an initial outcome, a mere first step. And he went on, "Mental illnesses, you know this better than I, are still shrouded in mystery, and therefore it's best to proceed with your feet firmly on the ground. Even Freud, the consummate master, was wont to say that each of us, even the healthiest among us—to use a conventional term—several times a day, perhaps without realizing it . . ."

In Augustus the Second, the bitterness of not seeing his proposal welcomed more favorably had produced, by way of a natural process, a self-destructive impulse: if things were going to go badly, they might as well go even worse. So he said, "That's what you told me the first time we saw each other."

Then he immediately bit his tongue because the consequences of his interruption quickly proved to be cataclysmic. Doctor Caroniti hated him. Augustus pulled himself together and murmured, "I'm sorry."

This simple phrase was all it took to make Doctor Caroniti return to his customary professional demeanor. "But no," he said calmly, "you mustn't ever apologize for anything. You must, no matter what, behave with the utmost spontaneity, say everything that comes into mind, otherwise how will I ever be able to penetrate your subconscious? So, yes,

I repeated myself on purpose, citing Freud, precisely to put you to the test, a sort of test in order to see your reaction. Unfortunately, you displayed impulsivity, a lack of reflection. And naturally, insecurity, psychic unease, and more. Then again, your behavior during your hospitalization, though in some respects quite laudable, in other respects has aroused more than a few concerns. Some disturbances are undoubtedly still present. You certainly don't mean to tell me that it is normal behavior to attempt carnal conjoinment on a bench with a patient in front of the other patients. Quite frankly, Signor Valle, I see your being released as cured as something unfortunately still a long way off. But being cured is not the only way to get out of a psychiatric hospital."

That said, that is, after offering this glimmer of hope, it appeared he had said all he was going to say. He remained silent, and Augustus the Second was afraid he was setting another trap for him, that skunk, to get him to fall into it and bury him once and for all. All the same, he risked it. "There are other ways?"

He'd guessed it; Doctor Caroniti immediately turned very cordial, albeit a bit didactic. "From psychiatric hospitals," he said, "it's possible to leave only by reason of death, about 20 percent of all cases, transfer to another psychiatric hospital, article sixty-one, being diagnosed as cured, article sixty-four, a minimal percentage, plus that's not your case, and finally, listen carefully, article sixty-six, about 40 percent give or take, in experimental family custody owing to improvement. Signor Valle, when circumstances are such that there are good family relations, I am willing to be liberal, even to take some risks."

By now, Augustus the Second understood where this guy was heading. "My family relations would be my wife?" he asked as prudently as possible.

He had guessed this, too. "You see," Doctor Caroniti said in total satisfaction, "you see, when you want to, you understand very well. Your wife is an extraordinary woman, positive, endowed with the practical qualities that are lacking in you. Give her the trust she deserves, Signor Valle. You won't regret it."

"I'll think about it," said Augustus the Second.

For Serafina, with her personal psychiatrist, things at the beginning had been even worse than they were for Augustus the Second. It was clear that they would never let her go. Asocial behavior and no hope of redemption. She was a total extravagance: she dressed like a hippie, spent hour after hour blowing into her flute, used language in a way that was nonsensical, believed in reincarnation, had difficult relationships with the female inmates and relationships that were all too easy with the male inmates. Even recently, unfortunately, in the gardens, with a half-wit male inmate . . .

"And what if I come to terms with my father?" Serafina asked at this point.

Her psychiatrist looked illuminated and relieved at the same time. He wasn't expecting such a sudden but undoubtedly advantageous change of heart in this darling patient of his. "Well," he said, "well, sure, if the distinguished gentleman were to agree, if he were to assume his part of the responsibility, if you should decide once and for all to be a respectful daughter, well, in that case, article sixty-six could come into play, experimental family custody owing to improvement. I, with prudence naturally, that is, after consulting with your father, could express a favorable opinion. I am a man of liberal views, I am opposed to total institutions, I don't believe that the asylum, in the long term, is beneficial to patients. And besides, you are not ill, remember that. You are merely a rebel, a malcontent, who unfortunately takes rebellion to a schizoid level. But now you're doing better, much better. I believe that the period you have spent with us, the treatment that we have administered, has been good for you. Ask to meet with your father, embrace him, tell him that you repent, show him the affection he deserves, poor man."

"I'll think about it," Serafina replied.

They thought about it together, she and Augustus the Second, by way of little notes that nurse Tommaso kindly carried back and forth.

The first to have a family meeting was Augustus the Second. It took place, as it did the other time, in the office kindly made available by Doctor Caroniti. Signora Palmira, it had to be acknowledged, was in fine fettle and, it seemed, well disposed. "Your doctor tells me you're doing much better," she said to him with a nice smile.

"I think I'm actually cured," Augustus the Second confirmed. "In fact, I want to leave here. What are your conditions?"

"You know what they are," she responded without missing a beat. "You sign over to me everything you own: the factory, the house, the gardens."

"And what do I get in exchange?"

"Speak."

"I want a separation and then a divorce."

"Agreed."

"I want my son, Giuseppe."

"Wasn't he Vigeva's kid?"

"Vigeva told me he's never made love to you because you're a prole and you stink."

"He stinks, like shit," Signora Palmira declared decisively. "He was born a redneck. He may have made a lot of money, but he's still a redneck."

"I want my son, Giuseppe," Augustus the Second repeated, not letting himself be distracted.

"Let it be," Signora Palmira conceded. "But I'll have the right to see him anytime I want."

"You've got it coming," he said. "Then I want a million lire a month."

"Are you crazy?" she scoffed. "The factory doesn't make a million a month."

"It did when I was running it," he said. "With all your ideas it'll make a lot more."

"Let's say half a million."

"Okay but indexed to the German mark. We always devalue."

Signora Palmira, even when it came to business, was surprisingly quick. "Agreed," she said, turning to go. "I'll be in touch with your lawyer."

"Just a minute," Augustus the Second stopped her. "I haven't finished."

"Now what?" she asked with a leer.

"The birds."

"What?"

"I want the birds from the gardens."

The signora's leer dissolved and turned into a smile. Now that she was about to lose him, she was beginning to find him amusing, this wacky husband of hers. "You really are crazy," she said to him with a gracious gesture of assent and farewell.

Serafina's discussion with her father went, unfortunately, much less smoothly. The big difficulty was the profound distrust that the distinguished Signor Bozzóli nourished for that wayward daughter of his, who, in truth, had given him fits time and time again. But she, in order to demonstrate right off the bat how much things had changed, went to their meeting dressed in dark blue, her pleated skirt just barely a mini, a blouse with cuffs and a white starched collar: a boarding school girl. The expression on her face was, as always, seraphic. She aroused an intense desire to be nice to her.

"Papa, you see, I'm a new person," she said as humbly as she could.

"What's that supposed to mean?" the distinguished gentleman asked incredulous.

"If you give me La Finca . . ."

"La Finca? And what would you do with it?"

"I want to go live there, far away from the world and people."

"You?" exclaimed her father, who figured she was telling him she wanted to become a nun or something similar.

But she explained, "I told you I'm a new person. I want to go live there with the man I love."

"You love a man?"

"For the first time in my life, I'm in love," she said sweetly but not without a pinch of emphasis.

"Actually, it's happened a number of times," her father observed.

"Not like this, Papa, I swear!"

"Let's hope so," muttered the distinguished gentleman. "And where did you dig him up, the lucky guy?"

"In here."

"A doctor?"

"No, a patient."

Her father gave a start. "So he's a loon!" he shouted. "I figured it was impossible! Forget it!"

Serafina didn't lose her composure. She kept her wits about her and played the affection card. "Papa," she said as soon as he had calmed down a little, "Papa, look me in the eye. How long has it been since we looked into each other's eyes, the two of us?"

It had been many years, actually, and her voice was tremulous, and as he looked into his daughter's eyes and she looked into his, the distinguished gentleman rediscovered a vein of tenderness that he believed had gone lost forever. For an instant, he even entertained the notion that money wasn't everything in life, maybe. "Serafina," he said.

"Papa," she murmured. She blushed. And she concluded, "Papa, I'm expecting a child from the man I love."

The distinguished gentleman started a second time, more intensely than the first. "Wench!" he shouted. "You'll abort!"

"No."

"I'll make sure you abort to the tune of kicks in the belly."

Serafina stiffened. She was suddenly ashen with contempt. She gave her father a last look and she turned to leave, saying, her voice shaking, "His name will be Bozzóli, like me and like you, because he won't have a father. Goodbye, Papa."

The gentleman didn't let her leave. "Wait," he called after her. He was trapped. "I assume he's penniless."

"He's got an income. We have everything we need."

"When are you going to be married?"

"As soon as possible. I mean, he's already married. We'll have to wait for the divorce to go through."

It would have been the case for the distinguished gentleman to give a third, perhaps definitive, start, but he was exhausted.

"Do what you want," he said. "Remember, though, that from me you won't get a dime. I don't let anyone take advantage of me."

"All I need is La Finca," Serafina replied. "After all, it's mine; you're not giving me a thing."

Epilogue

Ever after which, naturally,
some people will live
happily and contentedly.

It was, notwithstanding the current state of affairs, a beautiful spring day. In and around Milan, the sun was doing all it could to pierce the two hundred meters of fog-laden smog. Every now and again it succeeded, the sky suddenly lighting up and just as suddenly turning gloomy. Anyway, this was the day that Augustus the Second had gone to the gardens of the FIBA factory to pick up the birds, which, as agreed, he had the right to take away with him.

It was a day of frolic and detour for the innkeeper Giacomo Ballosta, for the local priest, for the town hall messenger Eriprando Bottecchia, for the municipal employees, and for the handful of other loafers in the town. The spectacle of the harvesting of the birds was definitely something to see. In the gardens, while on one side some hired hands had already begun sowing panic among the wildfowl by cutting down age-old trees, on the other, inside an enormous cage built on top of an enormous wagon, Augustus the Second, his little son Giuseppe, and that splendid lass Serafina, were busy calling the birds to salvation. Augustus the Second whistled countless calls, all of them perfect, Serafina blew into her flute inexhaustible trills and warbles, little Giuseppe twittered and clapped his hands, and by the hundreds and thousands the passerines and all the other species of birds swarmed into the cage, making, by way of celebration, a clamorous racket.

Naturally, inside the FIBA factory there was not a workingman or woman who was working. The new manager, Romeo, and the new owner, Palmira, said and did everything they could, but the workers would not return to their machines. They just stood there glued to the windows, looking out at the miracle of the birds and clapping their hands as a sign of their joyfulness and approval. They were all of a sudden on the side of their former boss, Augustus the Second, and they were all saying what a shame it was that he was going away, and they were also saying that he had found as his companion a lovely and properly refined young woman, not some dolled-up peasant.

Irritated and impotent, Signora Palmira retired to her living quarters, where she preferred to be alone, even refusing the company of bookkeeper Cusetti. She stood gazing out the window, looking at the wagon and that festive gathering of birds, and after a while she started to cry. She cried from anger, naturally, and from envy, certainly, but you never know, maybe her tears were also bitter because there is no heart so hardened that it can make a person immune to regret and melancholy.

So Augustus the Second and his seraphic companion Serafina, and the cheerful little boy Giuseppe, little by little gathered together all of the birds from the gardens into the enormous cage that had been built on top of the enormous wagon. Now they could set off. The enormous wagon naturally had an enormous tongue to which Augustus the Second yoked three pairs of oxen, which were indispensable to pulling the wagon. And once the six oxen were yoked to the wagon, Augustus the Second made a magnificent gesture of farewell to those who were looking on and applauding him, and he was just about to prod the animals to begin their noble labor when, out from Administration came scrambling, so to speak, Signorina Rosa. "Don't leave me here!" she shouted, "Don't leave me here! I'm all alone in the world!"

Serafina pulled her into the cage. She weighed less than a passerine, the poor old lady. Augustus the Second repeated his gesture of farewell to the onlookers. He even looked up to the window behind which Signora Palmira was concealed and flashed a look of beaming goodwill, then, no other impediments presenting themselves, he hollered to the oxen to move out.

The wagon got under way, slow and solemn, and the long journey began to La Finca, which was on the far side of Milan, on the way to the city of Pavia. Four days and three nights the journey lasted, on roads jammed with cars, bottlenecked by traffic lights, maddeningly entangled by one-way streets. The Milanese made no comments; by now they only had eyes and thoughts for their own affairs. Some thought maybe someone was shooting a film, but it was no concern of theirs. Just one gentleman, with the look of a colonel in the cavalry, who, however, was also a member of the World Wildlife Fund, doffed his hat as the wagon went by. And one little boy told a little girl, who was his special friend, that he had seen one of the wagons of Frederick Barbarossa, which perhaps had fallen behind on the journey to the Holy Land, but she didn't believe him.

It was before daybreak when they went through the piazza in front of La Scala, where there were only a few street sweepers, who protested because every now and again the oxen let drop one of those smelly road apples that the sweepers were not used to anymore. Augustus the Second tried to explain to them that the smell was a healthy smell, while the smell from buses was deathly, but they would not be convinced. So Augustus the Second let it lie and continued on his way toward the Tincinese Gate on the north side of the city. He had more than a little difficulty making his way through it because the traffic was becoming intense; half the people were trying to get out of Milan and the other half were trying to get in.

Then, beyond the gate, things started to go better, but it still took another day's journey before the city ended. Then still another day's journey before they arrived at La Finca. It was a vast tract of land full of trees and already inhabited by all kinds of birds. There was also a beautiful house, with a courtyard surrounded by a portico, and there, finally, the wagon came to a halt. The great cage was opened, and all the birds started flying about, free again, in a more beautiful sky.

Serafina, little Giuseppe, and old Signorina Rosa got down off the wagon and, holding each other by the hand, improvised, together with Augustus the Second, a dance of joy, like the ones the ancients used to do to celebrate nature. They were unmistakably happy and content, and so they remained ever after.

Notes on Contributors

About the Author

GIUSEPPE BERTO (1914–1978) was a great late-twentieth-century novelist who has recently come back to the fore.

Born in Mogliano Veneto, Treviso, in 1935, he was a volunteer in the Second Italo-Ethiopian War. During World War II, he enlisted to fight in northern Africa but was imprisoned by the Americans. During his captivity in Texas, he wrote *Il cielo è rosso*, a novel about the hardships of four teenagers after the American bombing of Treviso. Published in 1947, it quickly became an international bestseller. Berto then moved to Rome to work in the film industry. During this time, he wrote *Il brigante* (1951), and *Guerra in camicia nera* (1955).

In the 1950s, Berto suffered from severe neurosis and would recover only after many years of therapy. His condition became the core of his autobiographical novel *Il male oscuro* (1964), hailed as his masterpiece by many critics. Berto is a deeply modern writer whose unique use of narrative devices such as stream of consciousness and flashbacks has been labeled as a "psychoanalytic style."

Other notable works include *Anonimo veneziano* (1971), a short novel about love and death, and *La gloria* (1978), a novel based on the figure of Judas Iscariot.

About the Translator

GREGORY CONTI was born, raised, and educated in Pittsburgh and educated at Notre Dame (1974), Yale Graduate School (1976), and Yale Law School (1980). He has practiced law as a legal services attorney (1980–1985) and taught at Boston College Law School (1983–1985), the University of Perugia, and Rutgers (2013).

He moved to Perugia, Italy in 1985. His published translations include works by, among others, Emilio Lussu (*A Soldier on the Southern Front*, 2014), Rosetta Loy (*First Words*, 2000; *Hot Chocolate at Hanselmann's*, 2003), and Paolo Rumiz (*The Fault Line*, 2015). Most recently, he has translated three books by the plant neurobiologist Stefano Mancuso, *The Incredible Journey of Plants* (2020), *The Nation of Plants* (2021), and *Planting Our World* (2023); *The Child Is the Teacher*, a biography of Maria Montessori by Cristina De Stefano; (with John Cullen) the novel *The Color Line* by Igiaba Scego; and *The Seven Measures of the World* by Piero Martin.

About the Cover Art

Inspiration for the cover art, painted by Gus Rasich, a resident of Tennessee, comes from the following passage in Berto's novel:

Augustus the Second dreamed of himself and Serafina habitually. In his dreams, they were angels, or at the very least birds, who, as they flew along, sang the praises of nature and God, and just so, flying and singing, they satisfied, it seemed, all of life's duties.